JUDE BANKS, SUPERHERO

PENGUIN WORKSHOP
An Imprint of Penguin Random House LLC, New York

Emoji (used throughout): calvindexter/DigitalVision Vectors/Getty Images;
miakievy/DigitalVision Vectors/Getty Images

Visit us online at www.penguinrandomhouse.com.

Library of Congress Cataloging-in-Publication Data is available upon request.

ISBN 9780593094075

10 9 8 7 6 5 4 3 2 1

For Annabelle, Sam, and Grace,
loves of my life
—AH

JUDE BANKS,

SUPERHERO

by Ann Hood

PENGUIN WORKSHOP

PROLOGUE

If you asked me how I, a boy at the age of twelve, ended up in a police station waiting to get handcuffed and booked for murder, I would tell you about City of Angels, I would tell you about peanut butter and heart arrhythmias. I would tell you about Katie.

Everybody feels guilty when someone they love dies. That's a fact, Gloria says. She says everyone thinks they should have been nicer or paid more attention. Or called a doctor sooner or stayed home longer. But the person who really is responsible, can you imagine how he feels? How he relives every minute leading up to it, over and over like a movie stuck on PLAY, as if he could stop time and change the path of things, make it better, different, less tragic.

On the afternoon in question, I stood in front of the big brick police station, considering all of this—guilt and how you can't change things and how maybe this would finally stop that movie from playing. I had my toothbrush, some toothpaste, clean socks and underwear, and a shirt in my backpack, because I'd tried to run away from home. But I couldn't even get that right. I couldn't get anything right anymore. I disappointed people I cared about, people I cared about died, and the guilt and grief had become part of me, Jude Banks. I'd slipped out of the house unnoticed and walked down the street without a real plan except to escape.

I had a vague idea of going to the ocean, but I wasn't exactly sure how to get there. It was south of home, even I knew that, so I headed south, or what I thought was south by the position of the sun in the clear blue sky. But in no time I was hot and sweaty and still very far from the ocean. I stopped and reconsidered. What would I even do once I got there? In movies, people stare at the ocean and come to great realizations. But I wasn't sure that happened in real life. Plus, it took thirty minutes by *car* to get to the beach. By foot, it would take ten times that long.

Should I continue south, anyway? Change direction? I paused, backpack hanging off one shoulder, and reviewed the mess that was my life. No one expects a twelve year old to be in such a mess, but there I was. I wondered if my mother had noticed I was gone, and a stab of guilt almost took my breath away. In the almost a year since Katie had died, Mom had become a stranger—wild-eyed one day, quiet the next, sobbing all of the next. Dad told me about a famous psychiatrist who figured out the five stages of grief: denial, anger, bargaining, depression, and acceptance. What about guilt? I wondered. Shouldn't that be a stage of grief? Or maybe it never went away, so it wasn't a stage but a permanent state of being. Not part of the five stages at all.

To me, they sounded like a logical progression. Denial for a few weeks, then on to anger, all the way to acceptance, checking off little boxes as each stage got completed, like the first day of school list for school supplies. The memory of all those afternoons at Staples with Mom and Katie loading up a cart with notebooks and pencils and markers pushed its way into my mind. Katie always liked things that sparkled; I liked purple. Last year, Mom found a sparkly mini stapler and held it up to Katie like she'd found treasure. I could see them there in the aisle, Mom calling out to Katie and holding up that shiny stapler and

Katie jumping for joy, literally. Three big kangaroo jumps toward Mom, her head thrown back and her hair sticking up and her joy so real it was almost like something you could touch. I closed my eyes and didn't open them again until I'd pushed that memory way to the back of my mind. Since Katie died, I'd gotten pretty good at doing that.

That famous psychiatrist was wrong, I decided. Mom was angry one minute, then depressed, and then back to angry. Once in a blue moon, she was almost normal. But when that happened, it was a pleasant surprise. When that happened, I moved gently around her. The thing was, I never knew which mother I would find when I came home from school.

"Have you heard of the psychiatrist who discovered the five stages of grief?" I asked Mom one afternoon when she seemed as close to normal as she got those days, which meant a lot of staring into space but also that her hair was brushed and she was dressed in clothes that matched.

"Kübler-Ross?" she said.

Before I could answer, Mom said, "She got it all wrong, didn't she, Jude?"

I sighed. "Yeah," I admitted. "She did."

With a mother like that, how could I know what she would do when she realized I wasn't home? A teeny-tiny part of me wondered if she might actually feel relief. Without me to care about, she could stay in her pajamas for the rest of her life, drink wine for breakfast, not have to pretend things were getting okay.

I stared up at the police station. I'd only managed to walk two towns away from home. My feet hurt in their Converses, and I was tired. So tired that I wasn't sure I could make it up the big stone steps to the front door, though of course I did. Inside didn't look anything like police stations I'd seen on television. It looked more like an office, with regular people in regular clothes instead of uniforms and badges, everyone sitting at computers and typing.

A woman with lots of dark hair piled high on her head sat at the desk that faced the door. She was staring at her computer screen, too, typing fast. A black-and-white nameplate said HILARY HITCHCOCK.

I walked over to Hilary Hitchcock, my legs heavy, like they got when I'd been swimming too long.

"Excuse me," I said. My voice came out like a squeak.

"Uh-huh," Hilary Hitchcock said without looking at me, still typing like crazy.

I cleared my throat. I had to find my voice somehow.

"I need to talk to a policeman," I said, still all squeaky and small. "A sergeant, maybe."

She stopped typing and looked at me. Her eyebrows had been plucked off, and she'd drawn in new ones with a dark pencil. When she frowned, they looked like caterpillars moving.

"A sergeant," she repeated.

I cleared my throat again. Somewhere inside me was the voice of a superhero. Katie thought so. Now I had to find it.

"Someone in charge," I said. A little stronger? Maybe?

"You want to try me?" she asked, and she took out a clipboard and a pen like she was ready to write down whatever I told her.

"I can only tell a policeman." So he can arrest me and get it over with already, I thought, but obviously didn't say.

Hilary Hitchcock put down the clipboard, picked up a telephone receiver, and pressed a couple of buttons that lit up when she touched them, eyeballing me the whole time.

"Jeffers, can you come out here, please?" she said. "There's a kid needs to talk to you."

"He should bring handcuffs, I think," I told her.

She frowned deeper. "Yup," she said into the phone. "Yup." Then she hung up.

Hilary Hitchcock and I stared at each other until a door opened and out came a policeman—Jeffers, I guessed. I was glad Jeffers looked like a real policeman, with a hat and a badge and stripes on his shirt.

His very long legs marched right over to me.

"Officer Jeffers," he boomed, holding out his hand for me to shake.

I shook it.

"You needed to see me?" he said.

I studied Jeffers, his neat uniform and shiny badge, no handcuffs in sight. Still, I held out my hands, wrists close together like a criminal on TV.

"Book me," I said, and to my surprise, hot tears fell down my face.

"Book you?" Jeffers said.

I nodded. "For murder," I said. "Please," I said. "Arrest me."

CHAPTER ONE

The day before I killed my sister, she told me to drop dead. We had just read *Romeo and Juliet* in Honors English, so I was aware of the irony. In the play, Juliet tells her nurse to find out who Romeo is. "If he be married," she says, "my grave is like to be my wedding bed." Katie had to explain to me why this was ironic, of course.

For exactly twenty-five days a year, Katie and I were the same age. We were eleven months and five days apart, and if you had to guess, you would think Katie was eleven months and five days older than me because she knew more than I did, had a gigantic vocabulary, and in every possible way seemed like she was the oldest. But, in fact, I was eleven months and five days older than Katie— twelve to her eleven, except for twenty-five days in July that this year would not matter.

Katie belonged in Honors English. She loved to read, memorized poems for fun, and walked around dramatically reciting lines from Shakespeare in a fake British accent. She had skipped a grade, which was why she was in seventh grade with me. The teachers had wanted her to skip a grade last year, too, but Mom didn't want her with kids that much older than her. Someone like that, a grade skipper and a book lover and a Shakespeare memorizer, should be in Honors everything. I, on the other hand, was still not sure why I'd been placed there. Surely it had been a mistake, an administrative error of some kind. Mom said it was to show me that I was smarter than I thought I was. "You have as much to say as Katie does," Mom told me. "You just need to speak up." Still, I spent most of my time in Honors English feeling like an impostor.

"It's verbal irony because we know she's going to die on her wedding bed," Katie explained.

"We do?" I said. "How do we know that?"

"Because it's *Romeo and Juliet*!" Katie screeched at me, pulling at her hair. She pulled at her hair a lot because she got frustrated a lot. Especially at me, who was not as smart as she was and also liked to drive her to the point of pulling at her hair, which was short, red, and stuck out funny when she yanked on it. "They die! That's what the play is about!"

That time, though, I wasn't trying to make her crazy. I hadn't read the whole play yet. I just read the parts Ms. Landers assigned each night. I was not a skip-ahead kind of person.

"I thought it was about falling in love with the wrong person," I said truthfully.

Katie groaned—dramatically. "Act Five. Scene Three. Romeo sees Juliet and thinks she's dead when she's really only faking her death, and so he drinks poison, and then when she wakes up and sees him dead beside her, she takes his dagger and says, 'O happy dagger, This is thy sheath' and stabs herself to death on *her wedding bed*!"

This being Katie, she delivered all of this information in one breathless rush until she got to the dagger part, at which point she stood up and acted horrified to see Romeo dead, then slowly pretended to remove the dagger before she said "O happy dagger, This is thy sheath" very melodramatically, plunging the imaginary dagger into her chest and falling onto the floor.

"But, Katie," I said, standing over her as she lay

completely still on the floor, one hand clutching the dagger and the other swept across her eyes, "a person who doesn't know any of this, who's maybe way back in Act One, Scene Five, can't know that Juliet is doing verbal irony."

Katie didn't respond. Or move.

I poked her with my toe. "Come on, get up."

She moved her arm from across her eyes and glared at me. "You don't *do* verbal irony," she said. "It's a literary device."

"I just think—"

"Stop! You are being so annoying!"

"I—"

Katie jumped up. "Just . . . just . . . drop dead!" she yelled and stomped off, her hair sticking up like a cartoon electrocuted person.

"Sorry!" I called after her, smiling to myself.

My sister was so dramatic, so absurd, so funny, so smart, so uniquely unique, and I loved her more than anything in the world. I told her that, too, every night before we drifted off to sleep.

Mom told us that from the start, we were inseparable. Like peanut butter and jelly. Like Simon and Garfunkel;

Tom and Jerry; Fred Astaire and Ginger Rogers. All good things came in twos, she said. In some countries, she said, it was good luck to bring two mandarin oranges to someone you love. What would a person do with a bat but not a ball? Or one shoelace? Or a single chopstick?

Most nights, we still fell asleep next to each other. Yin and yang. All day, we squabbled and teased and rolled our eyes at each other. At night, though, we lay side by side on beanbag chairs or on the sweet summer grass or under down comforters, and we wrapped our fingers together and whispered our secrets to each other. We laughed about our fights, about our parents, about our cat, Sparkle. We made big plans—to sail around the world, not someday but soon, maybe even next week or next month; to live in a yurt; to write a movie, a play, a saga—and small plans, like going to sailing camp so we could sail around the world. Eventually one of us, usually me, fell asleep, and the other one, usually Katie, gently guided them to bed. "Who needs LMNO when you've got J and K?" we'd whisper to each other, an old joke from way back when we were three and learning our ABCs.

That night before I killed Katie was no different.

We stretched out on our beanbags, the ones we got the previous Christmas with our names printed on them, and we held hands and faced each other.

"I don't really want you to drop dead, Jude-o," Katie said. Only to her was I Jude-o, or Judy, or JJ, or Jinx.

"I know," I said.

"I'm sorry I read the whole play in one go," she said, with a big sigh. "I couldn't help myself."

"K-k-k-Katie, smarty-pants Katie," I sang softly. She was also Katy-did. Katzenjammer. KK.

"I'm sorry my brother is of inferior intelligence," she said, squeezing my hand.

"Jude of all trades, master of none."

"Do you think I'll ever be a famous actress, JJ?"

"Absolutely."

"And will I win the Pulitzer Prize for Fiction?"

"Most definitely," I said. "Also for Nonfiction. Also the Noble Prize."

"Nobel."

"Huh?"

"My dearest brother. It's No-bel prize. Not No-BUHL. Though it's surely noble to win one," she added kindly.

"But you'll win both. No-bel and No-BUHL."

"Lucky me," Katie said.

"Lucky you," I said, drifting off to sleep.

"Ya lyublyu tebya," Katie said softly.

I smiled. When we were in fourth grade, she'd made us both memorize how to say *I love you* in twenty different languages. She'd learned them all, plus ten more.

"Russian," I said sleepily. "Show-off."

Katie stood and pulled me to my feet. She put a hand on the small of my back and led me down the hall to my room. Without asking, she switched on the night-light, knowing I still woke sometimes during the night and was afraid of the dark.

I climbed into bed and managed a "Ti amo."

Katie kissed my hand lightly. "An easy one. But I'll forgive you on the grounds of sleepiness."

I wished I remembered if she had said anything else before she slept. I wished I remembered every detail. But I fell asleep immediately, and when I woke in the middle of the night, grateful for the night-light glowing softly, I wished I had just gone back to sleep instead of getting out of bed.

Life Before Katie Died

It was so ordinary. Mom, Dad, Katie, me, and Sparkle the cat. We loved one another, of course, but we liked one another, too. We laughed a lot together, and we played very competitive games of hearts, and Mom played actual records on an actual record player, and Katie danced with Dad, her feet on top of his feet, and Mom taught me how to do the jitterbug. We weren't allowed to do anything at the dinner table except eat and talk to one another. Our house was nothing special, except that Mom liked lots of color, so we had purple walls and green walls and red walls, and she and Dad had bought lots of art on their honeymoon traveling around Mexico, so there was lots of Day of the Dead stuff, which meant paintings of skeletons dressed like people in wedding dresses and tuxedos and very colorfully decorated skulls.

My friend Gilbert said the art in our house scared him, but we were used to it, and everybody had their favorite skeleton whom they got to name.

Dad worked as a landscape architect, designing parks and playgrounds, and Mom worked part-time at a college as a drama teacher. One year, she directed their spring play, *Oliver!*, and Katie and I got to be orphans and in Fagin's gang because they needed real kids, not just college kids who looked young. At the end of every semester, Mom had her students over, and she made her famous paella, and Katie and I got to pass hors d'oeuvres. At the end of the night, somebody always played the guitar and everybody sang and they all toasted Mom because she was the best teacher they'd ever had.

But mostly we just went to school, came home, and had a snack—apples and peanut butter or popcorn or Mom's famous peanut butter and jelly bars. We did homework. We played outside, even in winter, because Mom believed that fresh air was good for us. We bickered with one another. We made up. We ate dinner and played hearts and Mom read to us and Dad ran his ideas for a new park or playground past us and we watched one hour of TV and went to bed. Day after lovely day.

Life before Katie died was so ordinary that it was perfect.

CHAPTER
TWO

Ms. Landers made us memorize poetry. "Train your brain!" she said, as enthusiastic as a cheerleader or a drill sergeant. She told us about John McCain. He was shot down in Hanoi during the Vietnam War and spent five and a half years in captivity. "Do you know what kept him sane all those years?" Ms. Landers asked us. Before we could answer, she shouted, "Poetry!" Apparently, according to Ms. Landers, people who memorize poems do better as prisoners of war.

Ms. Landers was that perfect teacher who had high expectations for us but also liked to laugh and talk to us like we were real people instead of kids. She wore interesting scarves and big jewelry that she bought on her travels. "See the world!" was another thing she told us to do. Ms. Landers was everybody's favorite teacher, the one who had former students show up at school to tell her she had changed their lives or just to stand in her aura and get recharged by her high expectations. When she said, "Well done!" those words could keep you going for days. Of course, when she told you that you could do better, you felt terrible, not just because she was right but because you'd let her down.

Of all the crazy things I felt bad about when it came to Katie dying, I felt really bad that she died in September and only got to have Ms. Landers for three weeks. In that short time, it was already obvious that Ms. Landers adored her, was delighted by her. At the memorial, Ms. Landers held my mother and cried with her for a really long time. These were the kinds of moments that stood out from that terrible, unimaginable day. My English teacher hugging my mother and crying. Or how Gilbert stayed by my side the whole time, not saying anything, just being there, which was exactly what I needed. Gilbert, who was my best friend, went to a fancy private school and had to wear a tie there every Friday.

Or how I wanted to be one of the people who stood up at the front of the church and told everyone how amazing

Katie was, but when I saw all those people in black clothes, I got scared and couldn't think of one thing to say. Or how I saw Benjamin Hale talking to Ali Moffatt, and I got so mad that I had to go outside and walk around and around really fast until I calmed down, because Katie loved Benjamin Hale. Or later, how I ate three chicken-salad finger sandwiches way too fast and threw up in the bushes, Gilbert looking the other way while I puked.

Katie never got to train her brain. But I had to. The first poem Ms. Landers made us memorize was "Stopping by Woods on a Snowy Evening" by Robert Frost. I knew who Robert Frost was, but I didn't tell her that. I didn't tell her that my mother loves Robert Frost poems. I didn't tell her that the last words of his poem "The Master Speed" were carved into a pink-granite gravestone in the cemetery right down the street. *Wing to wing and oar to oar.*

I just memorized "Stopping by Woods on a Snowy Evening," which was a pretty nice poem about a guy and his horse and—big surprise—a snowy evening. When Ms. Landers started asking us questions like, "Whose woods *are* these?" I stopped listening. The poem said that the guy's house was in the village, which was good enough for me.

The next poem we had to memorize was "I'm Nobody! Who Are You?" by Emily Dickinson, a recluse who lived in the 1800s. The poem is full of dashes and exclamation points and it was super easy to learn, except for Henry Moorehead, I guess, because when it was his turn to recite the poem, he said, "To tell one's name – the livelong June – to an admiring *Blog*!" instead of "to an admiring Bog!"

"Henry," Ms. Landers said, trying not to laugh, "it's *bog*, not *blog*. There were no blogs in the nineteenth century."

Ali Moffatt leaned over and whispered something to Benjamin Hale and he smiled and I felt that same anger rising up inside me, like I could punch him in his face because Katie had loved this moron with his stupid hair always falling in his eyes and his big, dumb grin. I took deep breaths and forced myself to think about the poem and Emily Dickinson all dressed in white writing it.

⌲

Maybe I'd be a prisoner of war someday. I didn't think so, but John McCain probably didn't think he'd ever crash in Hanoi and be in captivity for five and a half years, either. So I memorized the poems without complaining. Until the third poem.

"Class," Ms. Landers said, handing out photocopies, "this week's poem is by William Carlos Williams. William Carlos Williams was a doctor and a poet in New Jersey in the first half of the twentieth century."

I looked down at the paper and saw with great relief that it was an extremely short poem.

Ms. Landers read it out loud, and it was the most ridiculous poem ever written. A guy ate somebody's plums, and he says forgive me, except you can tell he really isn't sorry he ate them. All I could think of were all the important things to write poems about, like war and love. Like kids dying. And this guy, this William Carlos Williams, was writing about plums? Eating someone's plums? It was too much for me.

"William Carlos Williams wrote this poem after he ate his wife's plums while she was asleep," Ms. Landers was saying, and I was starting to want to scream.

"And he left it for her in the refrigerator," Ms. Landers said, and she was actually smiling, like he was so clever.

All of a sudden, I felt so angry that I blurted, "That's dumb! I hate this poem!"

For my whole life, I had never been a blurter or a

shouter or even a person who spoke out of turn. Katie blurted and shouted and interrupted all the time. Maybe that's why I didn't need to. But ever since she died, I lost control, kind of a lot. Dad said I wasn't really angry about the things that seemed to upset me so much, that really I was angry because Katie died, and this was how it was coming out. I didn't know if he was right or not. I just knew that things like stupid poems made me so mad, I did or said things I never would have done or said before.

Ms. Landers looked so surprised that her eyebrows actually jumped way up on her forehead and her mouth made an egg shape, like a cartoon shocked person. Everybody turned and looked at me.

"This is a waste of time!" I shouted.

And then I ripped up the poem and I threw it into the air and I opened my notebook and started tearing out pages and ripping them up, too, and throwing them into the air. Some part of me knew that this was crazy behavior, especially over a poem. But I couldn't control it. I felt like something bigger than me had taken over my mind and my body and all I could do was watch myself act this way.

Henry Moorehead looked scared, like he might cry.

Ms. Landers came walking down the aisle toward me, and I threw my notebook at her. I missed, and it landed somewhere in the vicinity of her feet.

"Jude," she was saying softly. "Jude, it's okay."

By that time I was breathing hard, panting even, which made me think of bulls in a ring before a bullfight, how the picador pierces them with a lance.

I heard myself yell, "This is bullshit!"

Henry Moorehead did start to cry then, but otherwise the classroom was quieter than it had ever been, like the quiet on a snowy evening. I wanted to tell everyone that a good poem, a real poem, a poem that mattered was "The Master Speed." It was so important that its words got carved into a pink-granite tombstone. But Ms. Landers put her hands on my shoulders and was guiding me very gently out the door, still saying, "It's okay, Jude. It's okay." I didn't have the heart to tell her that it was not okay. Not at all.

Doctor Botticelli
Session One

One of the things they make you do when your sister dies is go to a *grief counselor*. Not just you, but everyone. Mom started going to Doctor Findlay practically right away after Katie died, and Dad recently started going to Doctor Madden, and lucky me, now I go to Doctor Botticelli. But only after fighting and hiding and throwing a temper tantrum the likes of which my parents haven't seen since I was three years old and they wouldn't let me get a pet lizard like Gilbert had.

"But Doctor Findlay is helping me so much," Mom said unconvincingly, because if Doctor Findlay was helping her, she would get out of her pajamas and maybe make us dinner. "Dad and I just want you to have someone you can talk to about this hard stuff."

"I talk," I muttered.

Mom and Dad exchanged a look like I wasn't right there in front of them.

"Doctor Madden says this guy is great with kids your age," Dad said, as if I cared what Doctor Madden thought.

For weeks, this conversation swirled around us with only slight variations. Until one night, filled with anger and grief and other emotions I can't even name, I went berserk and started throwing things around in my room— Transformers and complicated LEGO structures I'd built and framed family photographs—until Mom and Dad came rushing in, and Dad actually had to hold me down like cops do to bad guys on television. Mom just stood there looking at the mess and crying in a way that made me feel like she believed this could not be cleaned up. This could not be fixed. Which broke my heart enough to say, "Okay, I'll go to the stupid grief counselor."

Doctor Botticelli did not look like a doctor. He looked like a Las Vegas lounge singer named Dean Martin who Mom had a crush on. One of the things that Dad loved about Mom was her obsession with stuff from the 1950s. He called it *enchanting*, but Katie and I always rolled our eyes when Mom made us watch a movie with stars we'd never heard of or listen to her scratchy Dean Martin records. Doctor Botticelli had the same dark, curly hair and sleepy brown eyes, and even a voice like Dean Martin's, which Mom called *velvety*. I almost expected him to break into "Volare" or some other song that Mom used to play and dance around the kitchen to back when we were all happy.

"I'm not related to the painter," Doctor Botticelli said, first thing. "I've checked."

I just shrugged. I had never heard of a painter named Botticelli.

"The *Birth of Venus*?" Doctor Botticelli said, and he pointed to a framed museum poster of a naked woman standing on a scallop shell. "The goddess Venus arriving on shore after she was born," he said.

"She looks embarrassingly grown up to me," I said.

"Right? She emerged fully grown!" He shook his head. "Goddesses."

"Okay," I said, shaking my own head. This guy was a grief counselor? Seriously?

"You like art?" he asked me.

"I guess."

"Like who?"

I just stared at him. Who cared what art I liked? Wasn't I supposed to lie down on a couch? Weren't we supposed to talk about my feelings?

"Warhol? You like Warhol? All those soup cans and Marilyns?" he said.

Vaguely, I remembered a picture somewhere of a bunch of Campbell's soup cans repeated over and over.

"No."

"*American Gothic*? You know that man and woman holding a pitchfork? No? How about van Gogh? *The Starry Night*?"

"The blue swirls?" I asked him.

Doctor Botticelli got up and went to his bookshelves, which were a total mess. Books were jammed in at every possible angle, making a jumble of books. But he seemed to find what he was looking for right away, a big fat book that looked like it belonged in the library.

"Van Gogh, van Gogh," he said under his breath while he flipped through the pages. He started whistling softly, too, but stopped abruptly with a, "Here he is!"

"*The Starry Night*," he said. He put the heavy, open

book on my lap. On one page there was a picture of a painting of purple flowers. On the other side was *The Starry Night.*

It was the one I was thinking of, the one with blue swirls and yellow circles. In the bottom corner, there was a village and what looked like a scary black castle that seemed to jump out of the picture, but when I looked closer, I thought maybe it wasn't a castle but was trees instead.

"I like this," I said finally.

Doctor Botticelli nodded. "How about this?" he said, taking the book and turning the pages, whistling again until he plopped the thing back down on my lap.

The colors of this one were softer, almost blurry. A girl in a white tutu and ballet shoes stood, looking kind of sad, in what appeared to be a dance studio.

"It's okay," I said.

"Van Gogh is better?"

"I guess."

"What do you think about the girl here? The dancer?"

"She looks depressed," I said.

He nodded again. "Uh-huh. And this?"

ANN HOOD

He pointed to a picture that was definitely blurry. Blues and purples with water lilies floating on top.

"This is nice," I said.

"Peaceful?"

"Sad," I said.

Doctor Botticelli took the book and jammed it back onto a shelf.

"So you're a van Gogh guy," he said as he sat back down.

I shrugged. "Sure."

Doctor Botticelli smiled. "I like Venus up there."

For reasons I could not explain, I put my head down on Doctor Botticelli's desk and started to cry, hard.

He didn't do anything or say anything, but somehow his silence felt comforting, which was weird. When I stopped crying, he handed me a handkerchief that smelled like fresh air and had perfect creases ironed into it.

"You iron this?" I managed.

"Yup," he said.

"Weird," I said.

"Yup."

"Can I blow my nose on it?"

"Be my guest," he said.

After I blew my nose, he held out a straw basket and I dropped the handkerchief into it. Doctor Botticelli stood.

"See you next week?" he said.

"Sure," I said.

"See?" Dad said on the ride home. "Didn't talking to someone neutral about what happened feel good?"

I thought about the ballet dancer and the blurry pond and the starry night and that woman—Venus—standing on a seashell.

"Kind of," I said.

Dad exhaled like he felt greatly relieved. I decided not to tell him that we hadn't talked about Katie even once.

CHAPTER
THREE

"Hey, buddy," Dad said the night after the poem debacle. We were eating another dinner of another lasagna left on the doorstep. "There's this meeting tonight I thought I could take you to."

I played with the weird ground meat on my plate. I never knew there were so many kinds of lasagna. This week alone we'd had one with mushrooms and spinach and one without red sauce—LASAGNA: RICOTTA, MOZZARELLA, BÉCHAMEL SAUCE, the note taped to the aluminum foil said. Now this one with the strange-tasting meat.

"It's for kids who've lost siblings," Dad continued. "They meet once a week to talk about how they're feeling and stuff." He slid a brochure toward me.

Kids who've lost siblings. Like they've misplaced them the way Katie always misplaced library books and sheets of stickers and hair ties. If Katie were just lost, I would try to find her. No, I *would* find her, because I always found missing things.

"They even have a room where you can go and write whatever you want on the wall, and no one will see it." He tapped the brochure.

I looked at Dad. "Except the other kids who go in there."

"What?"

"If you write something on a wall, everyone who goes in that room can see it, can't they?"

"I guess," Dad said.

"Is this because of what happened at school? You think I need to get my feelings out in some dumb room?"

Of course, Ms. Landers had called my parents and they'd come to school to get me, both wearing worried faces. I'd been sent to the office—"Not because you're in trouble," Ms. Landers had said, "just so you can calm down a little"—and the secretary, Miss Nancy, had let me sit in the copy room and gave me some Hershey's Kisses. I stayed in there while my parents, Ms. Landers, and the principal talked in his office. If I had wanted to, I could have watched them; they were just across the hall.

But instead I carefully unwrapped Kisses and ate them very slowly, letting one practically melt away on my tongue before starting to take the foil off the next one.

After a while, Mom appeared in the doorway of the copy room and asked me if I wanted to come home or stay in school for the rest of the afternoon. I didn't care what I did, which sent her back into the principal's office for a discussion that lasted three more Kisses. "Why don't you come home with us?" Mom said when she appeared in the copy room again. So I did.

Now this.

"Maybe yesterday has something to do with it," Dad said, "but let's go to the meeting anyway?"

"I have mounds of homework," I said, pushing the weird meat around some more. "Including Earth Science, which is super hard." Wasn't Doctor Botticelli enough? Did I have to keep going to things to make me feel better? Didn't Dad know that this could not be fixed?

"We don't have to stay long. We'll just check it out."

"Did the note on the aluminum foil happen to say what kind of meat this is?" I asked.

Dad sighed. "It's not meat. It's tempeh."

"It's gross."

"They have pizza," Dad said.

"Who?"

"At the meeting."

Now it was my turn to sigh. "Fine. But I'm not staying long."

"Just until after the pizza," Dad said. "Deal?"

I thought about Earth Science. I thought about igneous rocks and sedimentary rocks and metamorphic rocks. I thought about the outer layer of Earth, the crust. Beyond the crust was space and beyond space maybe there was heaven. Dad was scraping the gross lasagna off the plates into the trash, and I could hear the theme music from the British detective show Mom binge-watched.

"In Australia, there's granite that's over four billion years old," I told him. "That doesn't seem right, does it? That stupid rocks get to be four billion years old?"

Dad was at the sink now, rinsing off the plates. He turned to me and said, "I know, buddy."

"Just until after the pizza," I said.

Dad only nodded, but I could tell he was relieved.

The group was called City of Angels, and they met in the same office building as my dentist, Doctor Wolfe. Not a good start, since I hated going to Doctor Wolfe. Plus, when we walked in, everyone was already sitting in a circle, looking miserable. A woman standing at the door said, "There's juice," in a stage whisper and pointed toward a table. Everyone stopped talking and watched us walk over to the table and pour some apple juice into small paper cups.

A girl who looked like she was in college came up to us. She had on a droopy, gray wool hat, even though it wasn't cold, and oversize black glasses. "Hi. I'm Gloria, the teen coordinator. Come and join us."

Dad started walking toward the group, but Gloria said, "The parents are in the room next door." She was short and had on big black boots like construction workers wore.

"See you in a bit, buddy," Dad said, and just like that he walked out.

Me and my apple juice found an empty seat in the circle, as far at the edge as possible. I never liked sitting in circles, even in school when we broke into reading groups.

"What's your name?" Gloria asked me. Between the

bangs and the big glasses, I couldn't even see her eyes.

"Jude," I mumbled.

"June?" Gloria said.

I felt my cheeks burn. What boy was named June?

"Jude," I said again, too forcefully this time.

Gloria laughed. "Okay, JUDE."

Some kids giggled. I stared at my Converses.

"Let's give JUDE a big City of Angels welcome, okay?" Gloria said.

"Welcome, Jude!" everyone said, sounding pretty lackluster. Who could blame them? A bunch of kids who had dead sisters and brothers wasn't exactly cheerful.

"Here are the rules about group in City of Angels," Gloria said. "Tell him, everybody!"

"There are no rules!" everyone shouted.

I wished I could disappear. I hated it there so much already, and I'd promised to stay until the pizza part.

"You can say anything. Say nothing. Do anything. Scream. Swear. Cry," Gloria said. "No rules. Okay?"

I nodded.

"We've got this angel, and when you want it, we hand it to you, and you can do or say anything you want when you're holding it. When you're done, you pass it on."

I looked up. Gloria was holding a vaguely angel-shaped doll. It reminded me of the stuffed cat Katie made in Brownies, except with wings.

"That's a rule," I said.

Gloria was turned in my direction, still wearing that dumb hat. I guessed it was, like, a fashion thing. I wondered if I ever came back, which I wouldn't, if she'd have that hat on again.

"We've got this angel," I repeated, "and when you want it, we hand it to you, and you can do or say anything you want when you're holding it."

The room was eerily silent, which meant all these kids really liked Gloria and thought I was being a jerk.

"Do you want to hold the angel, Jude?" Gloria said.

I shook my head.

"I do," a girl across the circle from me said.

Gloria got up and placed the angel in the girl's hands. The girl had long shiny hair, like she was from a shampoo commercial.

"I am so mad at my sister for dying that if she wasn't already dead, I'd kill her," she said.

Somebody started crying.

"Me too," the girl sitting right beside me said softly. She smelled like Christmas trees, which was nice.

"Every day I stand in Halley's room, and I yell at her for dying," the girl holding the angel said. "I mean, how could she just go and die like that?"

"But they didn't choose to die," a boy with bad acne said. "I know that if he had a choice, Brian wouldn't have died. He tried to fight it, but cancer was bigger than him."

The girl with the angel jumped up and started making these weird guttural sounds, like a mad dog, and she pulled and yanked on the angel like she was trying to tear it apart. After what felt like forever, she threw the thing down, hard, and kicked over her chair. She was acting just like I had in school yesterday. I kind of understood why she was kicking and throwing and growling. No one did anything or said anything. I wondered if I should go over to her, but just then Gloria picked up the chair and the angel and gently rubbed the girl's back until the girl sat back down.

"Do you want to go in the Crypt, Clementine?" Gloria asked. The Crypt was the special dark room where kids could be by themselves and kick the walls or scream or write messages in colored chalk "safely," as the brochure said.

Clementine shook her head.

"Man, it sucks, doesn't it?" Gloria said to the group. "How could they leave us like this? Sometimes they don't even get to say goodbye. They're just gone. And we're left feeling confused and angry and sad. How many of you feel angry like Clementine?"

Gloria raised her hand and almost everyone followed. Me and the pimple-faced boy didn't, even though I realized I did feel angry at Katie, and realizing it made me start to cry. How could you die on me like that? I thought. The girl who smelled like Christmas trees put a box of Kleenex in my lap.

"If you feel like it, tell them how angry you are," Gloria said. "I'm going to. Who wants to join me?"

Kids started jumping to their feet, and Gloria yelled, loudly, "I hate you, Rosemary! I hate you for dying!"

Their voices rang out and names fell from their mouths: *Madison, Fiona, Jimmy, Paige, Dylan, Jacob* . . . *I hate you!*

Katie, I yelled in my head. But I kept it to myself.

When we finally had the pizza and I could get the heck

out of there, I saw Clementine standing next to a sad-looking woman who had the same shampoo-ad hair. Her mother, I guessed. They were both holding paper plates with pizza on them, but they weren't eating the pizza.

"Okay, buddy," Dad said. "We can go if you want. But maybe we can come back next week?"

I was never coming back. Why would I want to sit around with a bunch of other miserable kids and act miserable and sad?

"One sec," I said to Dad, and then I surprised myself by getting a napkin and writing a note on it:

THE OTHER DAY IN SCHOOL, I WENT BERSERK BECAUSE THE TEACHER WANTED US TO MEMORIZE A RIDICULOUS POEM, AND I AM TIRED OF THINGS THAT DON'T MAKE SENSE.

I signed my name, and underneath it, I wrote my phone number.

"Okay," I told Dad, "let's get out of here."

As we passed Clementine and her mother, I handed Clementine the napkin. She glared at me, and I figured she'd just throw it away. But still I felt good, like I'd done something nice, one berserk kid to another.

Things I Would Tell You about Katie

What do you say about an eleven-year-old girl who died? That she might have been beautiful someday, when she got her braces off or finally stopped growing and stopped looking so awkward in her too-tall body. That she was too smart for her own good and too theatrical, always dropping to the floor dramatically or speaking in accents or wearing feathered boas and glitter. That she loved Shakespeare and Louisa May Alcott. And *Teletubbies*. And peanut butter and banana and honey sandwiches. And crunchy Cheetos but not puffy ones. She loved ancient Egypt and parades. She loved Benjamin Hale, but he didn't know that. She loved the old novel *Love Story*, which she plucked from our mother's bookshelf two weeks before she died. It's about a twenty-five-year-old lower-middle-class girl who falls in love with a rich boy from Harvard, and when they get married, his family disowns him. Then the girl dies, and the boy's father apologizes to him for being such a jerk, and the boy tells him that love means never having to say you're sorry. (I didn't read *Love Story*, but Katie acted the entire thing out for me about a million times a day.) (Also, I'm totally copying the way the opening paragraph of *Love Story* starts, except I'm substituting Katie-isms.) (Also, does love really mean never having to say you're sorry? I think about this. A lot.) From our mother's bookshelf she also loved: *My Ántonia, Jonathan Livingston Seagull,* and *Murder on the Orient Express.* She loved hot dogs better than hamburgers, baked potatoes better than mashed potatoes, corn better than any other vegetable. And me. She loved me.

Jude Banks, Superhero

Katie dropped things. All the time. She also lost things and broke things and forgot things, probably because she was always moving, fast.

"Jude! Help! My sparkly purple gel pen just fell in the crack between the wall and my desk!"

"I can't find the pin I bought when we were in Boston last year! The one with the cute sea lion face? From the aquarium? Remember, JJ?"

"I just broke my favorite bracelet! All the shells came flying off! Can you put them back on, Jude-o?"

"I forgot where I left my library book, Jude. The one about female pirates? It's due today!"

I would squeeze my hand behind the desk, search under Katie's bed and in her piles of stuff, crawl on the floor to retrieve errant seashells, and find the book about female pirates outside under Katie's favorite tree.

"You, my brother, are a hero," she'd say when I handed her the sparkly purple gel pen, the sea lion pin, the restrung shell bracelet, and the book about female pirates.

"No, I'm not," I'd say, my chest swelling with pride. "I'm just logical."

"You're right. You're not a hero. You're a *super*hero. I'm going to learn how to sew just so I can make you a cape with a big J on the back. You'll have to provide your own tights, however."

Superheroes rescued people. They saved lives. They brought order to chaos. Of course, Katie never learned how to sew—sewing required sitting still for way too long—but I imagined the cape she would have made me. It would have been red with a sparkly purple *J*. I imagined that with that cape on, I was taller and stronger and that I swooshed it with a flourish that would have made Katie proud. Jude Banks, *Super*hero, I'd think as I stepped into the path of danger. In my mind, I had a British accent, which gave me even more authority, more power.

Maybe if she had made that cape, I could have prevented what happened that night. But she didn't. And so I didn't.

CHAPTER FOUR

We were too old to still have our mother read to us, but we didn't care. We loved our mother's voice, which was neither melodic nor soft but husky enough that at least once a telemarketer called her *Mister* Banks, and her smell, which was not like flowers or cinnamon but more like the ocean on a cold day. We loved the ritual of her reading to us, the way we'd fit ourselves into her self—Katie propped up on her left so she could read along silently and me half lying down on her right. Mom is skinny, and we could feel her pointy shoulders and sharp hipbones, as comforting to us as our ratty baby blankets and the socks she warmed for us on the radiator on winter mornings.

Mom did not act out the stories or even read with much emotion. She just read out loud, pausing at commas and periods and raising her voice at the end of sentences with question marks. We liked to read everything by one writer before moving on, so she read to us all of Beatrix Potter (and Katie went around for ages announcing that the effect of eating too much lettuce was soporific, so she couldn't possibly eat any salad, to which Mom would reply, "Nice try, but you're not a rabbit so just eat your salad") and then all of Enid Blyton, and we were halfway through *The Phantom Tollbooth* when Katie went and died.

One of the things about reading with Mom was that she liked kids' books, even if we were too old for them or had already read them back when we were little. "You are never too old for a good book," Mom would say. Once she said, "Maybe reading all the Pooh books with you is a way to keep you young forever. Soon enough you'll be reading Hemingway and writers like that, and you'll be taller than me, and Jude will be shaving, and Katie will be wearing a bra, and—"

"Stop! We get it!" one of us said. Anyway, we loved Pooh and the Flopsy Bunnies and the Arnold family and, mostly, Mom reading out loud to us.

Sometimes we begged Mom to tell us stories about her life before she had us, when she lived in San Francisco and was an actress. "Well," she'd always say, "a waitress/babysitter/dog walker/barista/actress," which meant she had to work a million jobs just to try to be an actress. To Katie and me, Mom's life before us was worthy of a book or a movie. It was filled with fog and hills and a tiny apartment with views of the water and actor boyfriends. Sometimes we'd be watching a movie, and Mom would point to a guy in a crowd or at a bar and say, "That's Randy! My old beau!" And Katie and I would look at her in astonishment. Mom had beaus who were in movies?

Mom had long dark-red hair back then and big, soulful eyes; we knew this from a photo album that we sometimes forced her to show us. Mom on stage as Hedda Gabler, or a fairy, or in a garbage can doing experimental theater. Before she had us, Mom lived a whole different life, far away in San Francisco. Before Katie died, Mom was the mother who would let all us kids print neighborhood newspapers on her printer, make costumes for backyard plays Katie wrote (and directed and starred in), turn our whole first floor into a haunted house for Halloween parties, dye our hair blue or red or purple with Kool-Aid. She was the cool mom. The fun mom. The best mom. Now she was just the sad mom.

The Phantom Tollbooth still lay open, face down, on what we always called the puffy couch because it looked and felt like a big purple cloud. When we all three sat on it, it hugged us. "Please don't call it purple," Mom used to tell us. "Say aubergine. It sounds prettier." The puffy couch was in what we called the fancy living room, because all the furniture there looked fancier than the stuff in the rest of the house. The *aubergine* puffy couch, two chairs with uncomfortable backs, and a desk filled with secret compartments and drawers and an inkwell with no ink. The lamps were stained glass and turned on by pulling delicate chains. We mostly never sat in the fancy living room, unless our grandparents came for dinner and we all had cheese and crackers in there beforehand, or sometimes late at night our parents sat together on the puffy couch and drank small, delicate glasses of smelly liqueurs with French names. Or, of course, when our mother read to us.

That's where *The Phantom Tollbooth* stayed for weeks and weeks after Katie died, like the book itself was waiting for us to return. One especially sad night, amid all the especially sad nights, I asked my mother if she would read to me. I told her I just had to find out what happened to Milo.

"We can go on the puffy couch," I said, and for some reason I was whispering instead of using my regular voice.

Mom looked at me with wild eyes, like she was terrified, and she said, "Jude! I couldn't. I just couldn't!"

"Okay, okay," I whispered, reaching out and touching her arm. "No problem. Maybe we could read something else? Maybe *The Hobbit*? Gilbert read it, and he said it's really, really good." I was quickly learning that it was safer to do things with no memories attached.

Her eyes returned to their new flat, glassy state, and her body slumped, and she looked weary, like she was the oldest person in the world. "Maybe," she said. But I knew that what she meant was no.

Katie's Last Morning

We were late, of course, because Katie was always late. She was a "can't find my shoes" kind of person. Always looking for something she'd misplaced, or forgotten she needed, or she just moved slowly, slower than anyone in the world. Mom called her the Poky Little Puppy, like it was adorable to be so slow. "Dear me! What a pity you're so poky!" Mom would say as Katie, frowning, stared into her backpack or searched under beds and tables for who knew what. "Now the strawberry shortcake is all gone!" Mom would say, still quoting Janette Sebring Lowrey.

What I didn't know for sure, what I struggled to remember, was if Mom said that on the last morning. If I had known what was going to happen, I would have taken notes. Surely Katie moved too slowly. That was the only way Katie ever moved. I could remember standing by the front door, my ridiculously enormous, heavy backpack already on my back, ready to leave, to get in the car, to get to school before I would be marked tardy. I hated being tardy. I remember standing there, getting anxious about my impending tardiness. But had Mom actually said, as she often did when Katie was extra slow, straight out of *The Poky Little Puppy*, "Dear me! What a pity you're so poky!"? Why couldn't I remember *exactly* what had happened that morning, every detail?

It seemed extremely important to have a record of everything. Like what I'd had for breakfast that morning, for example. The last breakfast I ever ate with my sister. Cinnamon toast? Cereal with sliced bananas? An Eggo waffle? That was our mother's breakfast repertoire. Dinner was a different story. She'd make beef stroganoff or spaghetti carbonara or roast chicken with carrots and potatoes. She'd make strudels and crisps and cobblers for dessert. But not breakfast. Nothing special or creative in the morning for Mom, with her bed head and puffy eyes, pulling her trench coat over her pajamas. "I'm not a morning person," she'd explain if we looked at her weirdly or dared to ask if she could please, please, please get dressed before we left. What if we ran out of gas and someone saw her like that? "Fiddlesticks," she'd say. Before Katie, she'd say things like that, fiddlesticks or gadzooks. "Friends, Romans, countrymen," she'd say to us, "dinner is ready."

She didn't say things like that anymore. It was like her sense of humor, her smile, her special words had all died, too. How come when a person dies, a family's entire vocabulary changes?

I wanted to ask Mom that. I wanted to make her act like her old self. But I didn't have it in me to talk to her about any of this stuff. That first Halloween after Katie died, I'd gone into the basement and pulled out the bins of the haunted-house stuff. The person-size plastic skeleton that looked real. The cobwebs and rubber bats with big wings and glowing eyes. The cauldron and witch's hat and fake eyeballs and severed fingers. I had an idea to lug the bins upstairs and start decorating until, surely, Mom would want to help. But somehow, as I held up an eyeball or bat, everything looked so fake, so not scary, so silly, that I just put it all away.

One night, I worked up the courage to ask Mom about

that last day. She was sitting outside on the porch swing, wrapped in an oversize shawl, and I went and sat with her. I liked how autumn smelled; rotting leaves and apples filled the air. At first, we just sat without talking. The Carmichaels had put jack-o'-lanterns on their front steps, and they were grinning at us. Someone somewhere a few streets over was practicing the violin, screeching through some unrecognizable song.

I was surprised that Mom spoke first.

"I'm so afraid of forgetting her," Mom said. "I was sitting out here making mental notes about her."

"She was always late," I said.

"My poky little puppy," Mom said, and I could tell by her voice that she was dangerously close to falling apart.

"I wish I could remember that last morning," I said quickly, like I was trying to squeeze in words fast. "Like what we ate and if we talked in the car and—"

"No, no, Jude," Mom said. "We have to remember every morning. Every thing. Every single thing."

"Okay," I said.

"I'm worried that I've already forgotten something," Mom said.

"You haven't," I told her.

"But what if I have?" She squeezed her eyes shut and I figured she was trying not to cry.

"Mom," I said, "it's impossible to forget anything about Katie."

When she opened her eyes, they were glistening with tears.

"Katie is unforgettable," I told her, even as that last morning Katie was alive faded in my mind.

CHAPTER
FIVE

At first, in those days and weeks right after Katie died, Mom held me too close, clutching me and not letting go even when I tried to pull away. Sometimes I felt like I couldn't breathe; that was how close and how tightly she held on.

"You're all I have now," she'd whisper to me. Her breath, in those endless sad days, smelled like the coffee and wine she drank, which was a lot.

Those words terrified me. They made me feel like a precious, rare gem. Like the Hope Diamond that we saw in the Smithsonian on our family vacation to Washington, DC. Those words—"You're all I have now"—also made me feel heavy, like the picture of Atlas carrying the whole world on his back in Katie's beloved book of Greek myths.

Mom stopped eating, too. She'd nibble on a bagel or

some grapes, but a person can't survive on that. So Dad urged food on her, all the carefully prepared and delivered meals that neighbors and friends left for us at the back door. They arrived as if by magic in aluminum pans, wrapped tightly with foil and topped with instructions on how to best heat up or freeze the food. Some thoughtful people added details about the dish.

CHICKEN ENCHILADAS:
Heat at 350 degrees, uncovered, for forty-five minutes,

or freeze for up to one month.

Mild. Contains no nuts, but does have peppers.

Mom loved Mexican food, more than anyone else in the family. This was because when she'd lived in San Francisco in her mysterious Life Before Us, she'd lived in a neighborhood called the Mission that had tons of Mexican restaurants. We were okay with her making chile or burritos from time to time, but only because all the other dinners she made were our favorite things. Katie thought cilantro tasted like soap, which apparently was a real condition: "Cilantro contains a natural chemical called aldehyde, which is also used in the making of soap," Katie always reminded Mom. I didn't like anything spicy. So Mom adjusted her Mexican food to please us: no jalapeños, no cilantro, and as little onion as possible because neither of us liked onions. When Betty Carmichael left those enchiladas, Dad and I thought that after all the lasagnas and chicken marbella and ratatouille, finally she would eat something.

Betty Carmichael wasn't like the other mothers in the neighborhood. For one thing, she was divorced and single. There were a few other divorced parents, but they had all remarried new people. For another, she kept her blond hair super short, not in a bob or shoulder length like the other mothers. Also, Betty Carmichael had a job that sent her to places like China and Germany for weeks at a time, so that her daughter, Siena, was left with a college-student babysitter who fed her pizza and potato chips almost every night. We were extremely jealous of Siena.

Dad was working late, so I heated the enchiladas at 350 degrees per Betty Carmichael's instructions. The kitchen smelled just like El Coyote, the only Mexican restaurant around and the place where Mom always ordered the enchilada platter. I placed two on a plate and brought it into the family room, where she sat on the sofa with a glass of wine and her sad eyes staring at absolutely nothing.

"Mom!" I said with forced cheerfulness. "Look! Enchiladas!"

She smiled, maybe at my enthusiasm or maybe, hopefully, at the enchiladas.

I set the plate on the coffee table and placed a fork and knife and paper napkin beside it. Then I waited, willing my mother to eat.

She picked up the fork as if it were the heaviest thing in the world, and practically in slow motion dug into the bubbling enchiladas.

"Mmmm," she said. "Really good."

Silently, I thanked Betty Carmichael. I imagined leaving her a note begging for more enchiladas, an endless stream of them to feed my heartbroken mother.

She took another bite, chewed it forever, swallowed, and put the fork down.

"Thanks, buddy," she said.

I frowned. Two bites? That was it?

"Who brought these?" Mom asked, even though I felt

her attention drifting, felt her leaving me and going back to that dark, lonely Katie-less place.

"Betty Carmichael." I struggled to keep talking, to keep her here, but what else was there to say about enchiladas or Betty Carmichael?

"She's from California," Mom said, her voice growing small and drowsy. "That's why they're so yummy."

She refilled her wineglass and stared at nothing again.

"I used to go to this place in the Mission. La Rondalla it was called," Mom said, and I saw her eyes were filling up with tears, probably not over some dumb Mexican restaurant.

"No nuts, but they do have peppers," I said desperately. I didn't mention the cilantro or the onions, both of which I could see in there.

Mom surprised me by laughing, a short, bark-like laugh, like a laugh that hasn't been used in a while.

"That's what her note said. They all tape notes to the foil."

"How thoughtful," Mom said.

"Have some more?" I suggested.

"Oh, sweetie," she said. "I couldn't possibly."

She patted the spot next to her on the sofa, and I went and sat beside her. Just so she wouldn't clutch me, I began to eat the enchiladas. Betty Carmichael had said they were mild, but the sauce burned the back of my throat when I swallowed. Still, I slowly finished both, mostly to keep Mom at bay.

Later, I wrote a note on the monogrammed stationery Granny gave me the previous Christmas. Pale-blue paper with my initials in navy blue at the top and out of order, my last-name initial in the middle instead of at the end.

Dear Ms. Carmichael, I wrote after debating how to address her: Mrs.? Betty? Ms.?

Thank you for the delicious enchiladas. Did you know that Mexican food is my mother's absolute favorite kind of food? Like you, she once lived in California and has been a fan ever since. If you are so inclined, please bring her more. I understand that you are from California and therefore know how to cook all kinds of Mexican food.

Gratefully,

Jude Banks

I dropped the note in her mailbox on the way to school the next morning. To my great surprise, Betty Carmichael of the short hair and exotic job obliged, leaving an aluminum pan of carne asada burritos a few days later and more enchiladas—these with a green sauce—a few days after that. Mom did eat a little of these, more than of Mrs. Manning's vegetarian lasagna or the unfortunate veal stew Mrs. Van Buren left in her bright-orange Le Creuset. She'd taped a note to the lid that said: *Please return my Le Creuset! And enjoy this veal stew, heated stovetop until bubbling.*

As I sat across from Dad at the kitchen table, eating that stew and most definitely not enjoying it, I wondered if dinner would ever be normal again. Mom was in the family room taking small bites of burritos and watching her British detective show that had enough seasons to last practically forever, while Dad and I ate this overcooked veal stew in silence.

I looked at the table, which seemed to have gotten longer and wider since Katie died. It looked like a table that stretched across the room in a television mansion. I closed my eyes and tried to imagine the empty seats filled in—Katie across from me, Mom across from Dad.

I filled in the middle of the table, too, erasing Mrs. Van Buren's Le Creuset and adding a blue vase with yellow sunflowers, spaghetti carbonara in the red pasta bowl, and a green salad in the hand-carved wooden bowl Mom and Dad had bought in France. I added music, too, something bouncy like "Feelin' Groovy," and I added talking—Katie saying that lettuce made her soporific, and Mom's voice animated and excited as she described the funniest thing that had happened to her today, and me not having to talk because between Mom and Katie there was just enough talking, and Dad looking around, from Katie to Mom to me, and grinning at all of us happily.

"Jude?" Dad said. "Are you okay?"

I opened my eyes, almost expecting to find the very image I had imagined, a tableau vivant like I'd learned about in art class. Instead, I saw that Dad was chewing the tough meat and crying big tears. The only noise in the silent house was the theme music to the British detective show ushering in yet another episode.

Doctor Botticelli
Session Two

When I walked into Doctor Botticelli's office, he was sitting and swaying at his desk, eyes closed and music blaring. I stood there, unsure what to do. Why did I end up with such a weird therapist?

Without even opening his eyes, he said, "Like this? Ravel?"

"No," I said. The truth was, I didn't *not* like it. I just didn't want to be nice. I didn't want to be in Doctor Botticelli's office. I didn't want to be in grief counseling. What I wanted was my old life back.

Just like that, he opened his eyes and turned off the music.

"Huh," he said. "I like that. *Boléro*."

I stared right at his Dean Martin eyes.

"My mother has this thing for these singers from the

'50s. I don't know why, but she does. They're good singers, just old-fashioned. Frank Sinatra and—"

"Dean Martin, right?" he said. "I've heard it before."

"Oh."

"You like that music? The Rat Pack?"

"Who?"

"That's what they were called. Dean Martin and Frank Sinatra and—"

This time I interrupted him. "It's okay," I said. I thought about Katie singing "That's Amore" and dancing around the living room with the mop, and Mom laughing so hard she was literally doubled over. *When the moon hits your eye like a big pizza pie, that's amore!*

"Your mom has good taste," Doctor Botticelli said.

"She used to live in San Francisco," I said.

He laughed. "Well, that explains everything."

I didn't know what was so funny, and I was starting to feel even crankier.

"Have a seat," he said, and before my butt even hit the chair, different music came on, also really loud. But this music sounded like someone was being tortured or something.

After a few minutes, he said, "What do you think?"

"Sad."

He nodded. "Bach."

I didn't know much about musical instruments. Mom made Katie and me take violin lessons for a couple of years, but we both were so bad at it and made such a fuss about practicing that she gave up.

"You like the cello, though, Jude?"

"Is this the cello?"

"Pablo Casals, the greatest cello player that ever lived. In my humble opinion."

"I guess it's okay," I said.

"But sad."

"Yup," I said. Then I added, "I used to play the violin. But I quit."

We went on like this for what seemed like a long time. I didn't really like what he was playing, but he kept at it.

"Hmm," Doctor Botticelli said, "not a fan of Schubert's *Piano Trio Number One*."

"It's okay," I said.

It was all okay, but what I really wanted to know was what kind of grief counseling this was. What did listening to classical music have to do with Katie? Or me? Or anything?

"Chopin's *Nocturne Number Twenty-One in C Minor* not doing it for you?"

I shrugged. It all sounded sad to me, too, the weeping strings and repetitions.

But then he put something on, and I said, "I like this."

Doctor Botticelli smiled. "Not surprising coming from a former violinist like you. Also Bach. *Concerto for Two Violins,*" he added.

"It's like they're talking to each other," I said.

Before I even knew it was coming, there I was bawling again. This time in big sobs and heaves of my chest, snot running down my face. It was a two-handkerchief cry.

"Here," Doctor Botticelli said after I'd stopped crying and wiped myself down. "I'm texting you the link right now. *Concerto for Two Violins.* Play it at home if you want."

I just nodded because I was afraid my voice would come out weird after so much crying.

"Do you think you're making progress?" Dad asked on the way home. "I know you've only seen the guy twice, but is it helping?"

"I guess so," I lied.

Dad looked so happy that I didn't ask him how they'd even found Doctor Botticelli or what kind of weird grief counseling this was, anyway.

Instead, I closed my eyes and thought about those two violins talking to each other, one speaking and the other answering. It didn't make me want to cry, though. It actually made me feel kind of nice. Maybe Doctor Botticelli wasn't so weird after all.

CHAPTER
SIX

One of the weirdest things was walking home from school without Katie. We'd walked home from school together every afternoon since kindergarten, which was roughly one thousand three hundred times, minus days we were absent, which weren't very many because we were, as Granny always said when she saw us, "healthy as a couple of horses." One thousand three hundred times are a lot of times. We had our routine, our route, our pace. Sometimes other kids walked with us but not the whole way. We were always two by two, and all of a sudden I was all alone. Solo.

This afternoon I stopped and watched Siena Carmichael and her babysitter playing hopscotch in the street. Siena was giggling so much that I wanted to yell at her, *Shut up, please! Some people are not feeling especially happy!* Then I saw Mom, sitting alone on the porch swing, wrapped in that oversize shawl even though we were in the midst of a warm early fall day. The toes of one foot gently pushed against the floor to keep the swing moving. She was crying, the kind with tears but no sounds. I watched her, my ridiculously enormous backpack heavy on my back.

I thought about how Betty Carmichael had brought over nachos last night: *Just heat at 350 until cheese is bubbly!* I had helped a little by writing that note, hadn't I? Mom gobbled up those nachos, even making little appreciative sounds and wondering out loud if Betty Carmichael had actually made the refried beans on them herself.

You're not just a hero, Jude. You're a superhero! I heard Katie say in my head, which was the only place her voice existed anymore.

"Jude Banks," I whispered in a British accent. "*Super*hero."

I imagined growing tall, taller, as tall as the tree in front of the porch with its abundance of yellow and orange leaves. I imagined my muscles growing, popping up and out of my jean jacket. I imagined my cape whipping around me, and I swooshed it dramatically and flew into the front yard, up the porch steps, to my sad mother.

I extended my hand to her. "Let's go," I said.

She looked up at me with her big, wet eyes.

"It's imperative we go to the lemonade truck because it's the last day it's out," I said.

Some neighborhoods had ice cream trucks, but ours had a truck that sold frozen lemonade in green-and-yellow cups with a picture of a perfect lemon on them.

"Imperative, huh?" Mom said. The corners of her mouth turned up, almost in a smile.

She took my hand and let me pull her to her feet. I knew what grief felt like in your body, like you were made out of stone, heavy and unmovable. But I tugged her along until I could practically feel her lightening up.

The lemonade truck sat parked around the corner, a bored high-school kid stuck inside to scoop the frozen slush into the green-and-yellow cups.

I ordered a watermelon flavor, and Mom ordered a traditional lemon, both of us avoiding the mango, which was Katie's favorite.

We ate them slowly as we walked back home.

"Good," Mom said, squeezing my hand.

Jude Banks, I thought. *Super*hero.

CHAPTER
SEVEN

One of the many things Katie would have done, if she hadn't gone and died, would have been making flash cards for tomorrow's Earth Science test. Katie loved note cards and colored pens, file folders and highlighters. She could use all of these for her flash cards so that questions were color coded and subdivided. But there I sat, no flash cards and the test looming in a mere sixteen hours.

How are metamorphic rocks formed? Metamorphic rocks are formed by heat and pressure.

How are igneous rocks formed? Igneous rocks are formed by volcanoes.

How are sedimentary rocks formed? Sedimentary rocks are formed by years and years of sediment compacting together and becoming hard.

I wondered what kind of rock I would be if I were a

rock. Was I becoming hard? Was I under pressure? No. I was an igneous rock, formed by the volcano known as Katie dying, the top getting blown off my world and an enormous hole left behind.

All of a sudden, Dad was standing in front of me.

"So," he said, "it's Wednesday."

Rocks, I read, *are constantly changing. It takes millions of years for rocks to change.* Not very hopeful for me.

"City of Angels?" Dad said.

I held up the diagram Mrs. Carpenter had given us of the rock cycle.

"Earth Science test," I said.

Dad took the diagram and studied it. "Did you know that the word *igneous* comes from *ignis*, which is Latin for fire?"

"That's not on the test."

"We can leave right after pizza, and I'll quiz you when we get home," Dad said.

One thing to note is that rocks don't always follow this cycle. They can change from one form to another in any order at all.

"If we go now, we can catch the beginning," Dad said.

"We missed that last time. And I'm curious about what they do at the start."

Out of nowhere, like a ghost, Mom appeared next to Dad. She had on lipstick. And her nice coat.

"Let's go see what this is all about," she said.

They both had on their most concerned faces. How could I say no?

❧

When we got there, that same nervous woman was standing by the door. "Welcome back!" she said in a too-enthusiastic voice.

Did she know that some rocks came from space? That those space rocks were made of iron?

"Jude, right?" she said, and before I could answer, she wrote JUDE in green marker on a stick-on nametag.

When I just stared at it, Mom took it and slapped it on my shirt. Dad made nametags for him and Mom: BILL. SUSAN. Such parent names, Katie used to say. Gloria was motioning me over to the juice table, where a gaggle of sad kids hovered.

"Go on," Mom said, "don't worry about us."

"I'm not," I mumbled. They weren't the ones who

had to sit in a circle and pass an angel around instead of studying for an Earth Science test.

"Hi!" Gloria said. She did have on that same gray wool hat, I noticed right away. "Have a cookie. I made them from this famous recipe on the internet, and there are pretzels and granola in them."

I took a cookie and a cup of juice and stood there awkwardly like everybody else. There was the girl who smelled like Christmas trees and the pimple-faced boy and a few other kids who looked vaguely familiar. No Clementine, I realized, surprised by how disappointed I felt. Of course she hadn't called me. I looked her up on the membership list. She was fourteen years old, in the ninth grade, which was high school. Why would she want to call a twelve-year-old kid? She had probably crumpled up that napkin and thrown it into the trash.

"Okay, Jude," Gloria said, "what we usually do is mingle for about ten minutes, eat cookies, et cetera, then we go into the circle and do a little ritual that helps us get started on the right foot. Does anyone want to tell Jude how we start?"

A girl who was about a hundred feet tall looked down

at me and said, "We sit in the circle, and we hold hands, and on the count of three, we all say our brother's name."

"Or sister," the Christmas-tree girl said.

"Our sibling's name," Gloria said. "It's a good way to remind ourselves why we're here and to honor our sibling. I bet you've noticed that lots of people are hesitant to say your sibling's name? Right? What's your sibling's name, Jude?"

"Um. Katie."

Gloria smiled. "Okay. Katie. Here at City of Angels, we make a point of saying our siblings' names. My sister is named Rosemary. Rosemary drowned when she was six and I was eight."

"I'm sorry," I mumbled. There were so many sad stories in the world that sometimes I wanted to hide under my bed and not come out. Like now.

"Then we go around the circle and just share how our week has been, you know? But if you don't want to say anything, you just shake your head. No pressure here, Jude."

I wondered why I felt so much pressure then, like everybody was staring at me and my brain was buzzing with whether or not to tell everybody how this week had been. Maybe I was a metamorphic rock after all, created under great pressure.

"Then we pass the angel," Gloria was saying. "Oh! Clementine! Hi!"

I turned toward the door, where Clementine and her mother with the shampoo-ad hair were walking in.

"Get a cookie and some juice, and let's get started," Gloria said.

The really tall girl kind of glommed on to me. "I think ultimately coming here helps," she said.

I stared up the great length of her. It must be terrible to be that tall.

"It's good to know that I'm not alone, you know? Because sometimes I feel like a freak. The kid whose sister died in a skiing accident."

"Really?" I said. "That's awful."

The girl nodded. Her nametag said Tara.

"I just feel everybody at school staring at me, you know? But here, we all have equally sucky lives."

That made sense to me. I nodded. I kind of wished she'd leave my side so that maybe Clementine would end up sitting next to me. But no. I was stuck between

Tara and Christmas-tree girl—whose name turned out to be Holly, a coincidence that was not wasted on me. Clementine was all the way on the other side of the circle, and I consoled myself that at least this way I could see her very clearly.

I just sat there the whole time, thinking about rocks and shaking my head and keeping away from the angel. Finally, the circle thing was over, and it was time for the pizza part of the evening. All the parents came in, chattering away like they were old friends. Tara stuck by me all the way to the pizza, and just when I thought I might run out of there, Clementine joined us.

"I lost the napkin," she said, which made me blush really hot. She held her arm out. "Write it here. I probably won't lose my arm."

Tara stuck her arm out, too. "Me too," she said to me.

Clementine handed me a Sharpie, and I wrote my name and number on her arm, then on Tara's arm.

Then we just stood there and chewed our pizza, which didn't taste like anything at all.

Jude Banks, Superhero

They are walking down the sidewalk. Four of them. Mother, father, daughter, son. The mother has red hair and so does the daughter, and they are holding hands, walking way ahead of the father and son. I don't think the mother is happy. Her mouth is pulled into a tight, straight line, and she's frowning. But the daughter doesn't seem to notice. She's half skipping and half walking and her shoes light up with every step she takes. I wish she didn't have those shoes on. They distract me. They make me feel sad.

The father has the little boy on his shoulders. The father is tall but doughy, like he sits around a lot. The kid has red hair, too. Only the father doesn't, which I find weird because red hair is a recessive gene, so how did three quarters of the family get it? In our family, only Katie got it, and she got it from my mother's mother. The kid is eating something, maybe a lollipop. This is dangerous because if the father trips or falls, the hard part of the lollipop could come off, and the kid could choke. I consider stopping them and telling them this. I heard about a kid whose mother gave him a plum when he was in his car seat, and she drove to the grocery store, and when they got there, he was dead. Choked on the plum. You don't give a kid something big like that. You just don't.

"Hey," I say, kind of softly.

The mother just keeps walking and frowning, and the girl just keeps skipping, her shoes lighting up with every step.

"Hey," I say again. This time I say it too loud, and even the little girl looks over her shoulder at me. But I have to save that little kid. I have to save them all.

The father kind of leans down to see me better. His stomach hangs over his belt a little when he does that.

"You okay?" he says. His hair is the opposite of red. It's dark and very black.

The boy on his shoulders looks at me, and that's when I see that he doesn't have a lollipop. He has a flower.

A purple flower, maybe a violet. He grins at me and he holds out the flower to me, like a gift.

"You okay?" the father says again.

I want to knock that flower out of the kid's hand. I want to tell the father about plums and lollipops, just in case he doesn't know. But all I do is nod and turn around and start walking up the sidewalk toward home so they don't see me when I start to cry.

CHAPTER EIGHT

The diner was invented in Rhode Island in 1872 by a man named Walter Scott. Scott used to sell food in downtown Providence out of a basket when he was only seventeen years old. Business was so good that he parked a horse-drawn wagon outside the *Providence Journal* building and inadvertently invented the first diner. I know this because I was working on a research paper about diners.

I had my outline finished:

I. What Is a Diner?

II. The First Diners

III. The Diner and World War I

IV. The Diner and World War II

V. The Diner Post World War II

VI. The Decline of the Diner

VII. The Diner in Modern Times

"This," Katie told me, "is a very bad outline."

"I think it's perfect," I said.

"Under each roman numeral, you need subheadings marked by letters, and sub-subheadings marked by regular numbers. Like, under roman numeral I, you should have A: Invention of, and then number one: Where, number two: Conditions that led to—"

I took my outline from her. There was no way I was going to add subheadings and sub-subheadings. Things like this reminded me why Katie had skipped a grade. She pulled out one of those clear folders with the thin plastic bars up the side (hers was lime green) and showed me her outline for her paper, "The History of Musical Theater."

It was two pages long, and thick with words and letters and numbers and roman numerals. I couldn't even take it all in. I saw *I. Ancient Greece* and *II. The Renaissance, A. Commedia dell'arte.* I saw that Gilbert and Sullivan had tons of subheadings, like *H.M.S. Pinafore* and *The Mikado* and *Dorothy*, which had its own subheading of *Record-Breaking Performances.*

"Note the subheadings," she said.

"Uh-huh," I said.

Luckily, Dad walked in then, ready to take us to the Modern Diner in Pawtucket. For my paper, he was taking me to all the diners in Rhode Island. Or at least most of them.

"Are you going to take me to see *Hamilton* for research?" Katie asked him as we drove to the diner.

"Katie, tickets to *Hamilton* are hundreds of dollars," Dad reminded her. They'd had this conversation before.

"But I did a cost analysis," she said, pulling out another one of those folders (plastic-bar thing bright blue). "If we spend thirty dollars eating at diners every Saturday for five weeks, getting one ticket to *Hamilton* is equal to Jude's research expenditures."

"Hmm," Dad said, taking a quick glance at the folder in her hand.

"I've included the cost of gas and tolls," she added.

I could see Dad trying not to smile. He was always delighted by Katie's logic, her resourcefulness, her Katie-ness.

"I'll take it under advisement," he said.

Katie leaned back, satisfied.

Dad always did something special with us on Saturdays so Mom could have time just for herself. She might go and get the gray dyed out of her hair, or have her toenails painted baby blue, but mostly she just curled up with a book or worked on the blankets she was knitting for when Katie and I went to college. She was a very slow knitter, so she'd started when we were seven. Neither of us thought she'd finish by the time we were eighteen, but we always made a big deal of how much progress she made, how soft they were, how lovely the colors. She'd let us pick out the yarn. Katie picked hot pink and orange; I picked lots of shades of purple.

Before my diner research paper, Dad had us take turns deciding what we'd do on Saturdays. Katie liked going to the RISD Museum and staring at the giant bust of Buddha. I liked walking on the beach. I kept all the shells I collected from those walks in the lamp by my bed. It had a clear, empty base meant to be filled with something, so I put my shells there. Katie had an identical lamp, but she never put anything in hers. "I'm waiting to figure out the most perfect, the most beautiful thing," she always said.

When we got to the Modern Diner, I took a bunch of pictures of it, first outside and then inside, and then took notes about it from the back of the menu. *Customized and factory built, it is a Sterling Streamliner* . . . While I was busy with all that, Katie tortured herself—and us—about what to order.

"I should have the most diner-y thing, right? For authenticity?" she fretted.

"Get whatever you want," Dad said. "Don't sweat it."

"Corned-beef hash, maybe? Except I *loathe* corned-beef hash." She clutched at her hair.

"How about eggs Benedict?" Dad suggested. "That's your favorite."

"That's brunch food!" Katie said, looking at him with horror.

"Isn't it technically brunch?" Dad said.

"We're in a diner! For research!" Katie groaned.

The waitress appeared. She looked like she'd been working there since it had opened in 1941.

"Know what you want?" she asked us, already glancing over at other tables.

"Custard French toast," I said.

"Cheese grits, eggs, side of bacon, more coffee," Dad said.

We both stared at Katie, hidden behind the giant menu.

"Sweetheart? You ready?" the waitress said. Her nametag read NATALIE, but she didn't look like a Natalie to me.

Katie lowered the menu. She looked at Natalie's nametag. "Natalie," Katie said in her polite voice, "what is the most typical diner fare available?"

"Huh?" Natalie said.

"The most authentic diner fare," Katie said.

"Like, the most popular?" Natalie said, glancing at her other tables again. They wanted more coffee, or to order, or to pay up. "The custard French toast. Like this guy ordered."

"Custard French toast?" Katie said, her eyes wide. "That's too contemporary to be authentic diner fare."

"Sweetheart," Natalie said. "Just order. Please."

"Corned-beef hash," Katie said, defeated.

Relieved, Natalie scurried off.

"By next week I'll have done some research," Katie

said. "I'll be more prepared." She glared at me. "You're welcome, by the way," she said. "At least one of us is doing actual research."

Next week, we were going to go to the Miss Cranston Diner. Except, Katie died instead.

Things We Didn't Do Because Katie Died

See *Hamilton.*

Go on a summer vacation. (We were a family that always went on a summer vacation but never anywhere fancy or far away. Instead, we got in our car and drove to rented houses on Cape Cod or in Maine; to historical sites like Washington, DC, or Colonial Williamsburg; to classic places like Niagara Falls or New York City. Katie always made a PowerPoint presentation in the spring to try to convince our parents to go somewhere exciting, for once, *please, please, please.* These included Switzerland, Antarctica, the Amazon rain forest, and Kangaroo Island in Australia. Obviously, they didn't work.)

See Katie's PowerPoint presentation on where we should go for our summer vacation. Evidence indicates she was going to make a big push for England. She had neon

Post-it notes marking info on Shakespeare's birthplace, the London Eye, and Stonehenge. Though, Katie being Katie, she may have decided to read up on everything about England, just for fun.

Have Thanksgiving at Granny's. Mom couldn't do it. "I can't be with other people," she said. "I just can't." Every year of my entire life, I ate Thanksgiving dinner at Granny's in her house in Concord, Massachusetts, that looked like it was built for the sole purpose of hosting Thanksgiving. It was brown with an orange door. All the leaves on all the trees around it turned perfect autumn colors, and most chose to stay on the branches until after Thanksgiving. Every doorstep on her street had pumpkins and gourds artfully arranged, and the neighbors hosted a post-meal touch-football game where we all rolled around in the leaves that had decided to fall and breathed in crisp autumn air and then drank apple cider. Around Granny's table were vague relatives who we never saw except at Thanksgiving—the guy who pretended to remove his thumb, the guy who pretended to steal our noses, the woman who crocheted weird sweaters and tams to put on spare rolls of toilet paper. You could depend on the fact that there would be sweet potatoes topped with marshmallows, green beans almandine, oyster stuffing, glazed carrots, and six different pies: apple, cranberry, pumpkin, pumpkin cheesecake, pecan, and the mysterious dreaded mincemeat. But because Katie died, the three of us stayed home and ate a roast chicken that was not as festive and delicious as Dad kept insisting it was and a store-bought apple pie that Mom got at the last minute because we had to have dessert, didn't we?

We didn't laugh at Dad's bad Christmas sweater the whole week before Christmas.

Or watch Mrs. Carmichael giggle after she drank too much of Mom's special eggnog.

Or go into Mom's closet and look at all our Christmas presents.

Or read *A Christmas Carol* out loud, with Katie playing every part except the ones no one cared about.

We did not notice New Year's Eve come and go.

CHAPTER NINE

"Let's write our last will and testaments," Katie said. This came out of the blue, about a month before she died.

I was deeply involved in watching *Home Alone* for the third time. The cleverness of that kid Kevin fascinated me. If my parents and Katie got stuck in Paris, would I be able to outwit robbers like that? Probably not.

"I bequeath everything of mine to you. Except Sparkle," Katie said. "Because eventually you'll grow up and go away to college, maybe even do a year abroad somewhere like England or China, and what will become of Sparkle?"

"Okay," I said.

I loved the part when Kevin sets the booby traps. Katie had a way of forcing me to do things I did not want to do and of interrupting the things I did want to do.

"Aren't you even going to fight for Sparkle a little?" Katie demanded.

She had smears of blue and green paint on her cheek and her overalls, which somehow made her look younger. I thought about when we were kids and she'd make me lie down on a giant piece of paper and trace my outline, then paint it crazy colors and glue glitter all over it. *Now you do me,* she'd say, and I'd trace her outline but have absolutely no idea how to fill it in. I was someone who stayed inside the lines, and that big, blank Katie shape left me intimidated. While she painted splatters of bright paint all over my outline and threw silver glitter where my hair should be, I carefully painted blue overalls on hers, and a thin-striped shirt. It was laborious and uninspired. *Done!* she'd shout, and she'd step back all covered in glitter and paint, satisfied with the wild Jude she'd created. Then she'd see me slowly drawing wavy stripes where her shirt should be, and she'd scream, *Is that how you see me, Jude? Am I really that dull?*

"I mean," Katie said, planting herself between me and *Home Alone*, "we've had that cat since she was an adorable kitten."

I sighed. "I think Mom and Dad should keep Sparkle because I will not be able to take a cat with me to China. There are international laws that prevent that."

She grinned. She had me again.

"And?" she asked.

"And I bequeath everything to you except my Pokémon cards, because you hate Pokémon and think it's for morons. I'll leave those to Gilbert."

"This is an outrage!" Katie shrieked. "What if Pokémon cards become extremely valuable, and you have left Gilbert the equivalent of a million dollars? While I'm starving in a dingy apartment in Paris, possibly without shoes or even a coat, Gilbert—who is already rich—will be buying a yacht and sailing the Mediterranean with movie stars. Is that what you want?"

She had her hands on her hips, and her nostrils were flared like a bull about to run at a matador.

"Okay," I said. "If you promise not to destroy them, I'll bequeath them to you."

"Why would I destroy them?" she shrieked louder. "Just because I don't play with stupid things doesn't mean I would destroy them. I'm not a destroyer."

"You'll have to sign something that promises you will treasure them and take good care of them forever."

"Fine."

"And have it notarized," I added, knowing I was pushing too far.

"Fine! But because you are being such a . . . a . . ." I watched her struggle to find the worst insult she could. "Nitwit . . . I'm not going to let you come into business with me."

I thought she'd come up with something better than *nitwit*, but I knew better than to point that out.

Before I could ask what business she was in, Katie stomped out of the room. I went back to *Home Alone*. But not for long. Katie reappeared in no time, dragging a big sign across the family-room floor. I tilted my head so I could read what she'd painted on it: FREE ADVICE FOR $1.

"Katie? Free advice is free, not a dollar," I said.

She didn't even pause. She just dragged that sign out of the room. I heard it bumping along the floor, then I heard the door open and listened as she dragged it outside, down the front stairs, and to—I supposed—

her usual spot on the sidewalk under the shade of the Holms' giant oak tree next door. That was where she ran all her businesses: lemonade stand, baby-carrot stand, haiku stand, Shakespeare-quotes stand.

Later, when I was cutting up apples for my mother's famous apple pie and Mom was rolling out the dough, Katie came into the kitchen. She smiled smugly, reached into her pocket, and slapped money—coins and bills—onto the counter in front of me.

"Fourteen dollars!" she announced. "For my free advice!"

Mom chuckled beside me.

"One lady gave me *two* dollars because I told her she should get contact lenses." She waited for a response, but when she got none, she continued. "She told me she was ready for a *big change.*"

I decided to ignore her.

"I told another lady who felt she was losing her pizzazz that she should wear more blue, to complement her eyes, and another lady who was on the fence about getting a pet that, yes, she should get a cat. They make very good company." Katie looked very smug.

"All good advice," Mom said. "Look at how Sparkle has improved our lives."

We all glanced over at Sparkle, splayed on the tile floor like a small, furry rug.

"I know," Katie said. "Although I wish someone had asked me for a more life-and-death decision. Like, should I murder my wife or should I rob a bank."

"No one is going to ask a kid stuff like that," I said, ignoring my own decision to ignore her.

I sprinkled the apples with sugar and cinnamon and a squirt of lemon. "Maybe I should become a chef," I said, admiring my evenly sliced apples, dusted and shining with sugar and spice.

"That's a terrible idea," Katie said. She held out her hand.

"What?"

"You owe me a dollar," she said. "For my free advice."

"I wasn't asking for your free advice," I said. "Besides, even if I were, free advice is *free*!"

Katie glared at me. "I have decided to bequeath my bottle-cap collection to Melissa Burns."

"You don't even like Melissa Burns!" I said. "Plus,

I collected half of those bottle caps."

"Half? I don't think so."

"Okay, okay," Mom said. "Get this money away from our dessert, and both of you go wash your hands. No one's bequeathing anybody anything."

"Harumph," Katie said, which was one of her favorite words.

"Remember at the beach that time?" I said. "I found all those weird bottle caps? Like *cream* soda? And *birch beer*?"

Katie hooted. "And sarsaparilla?"

I was laughing, too, and we linked arms and left the kitchen to wash our hands, forgetting all about free advice and last wills and testaments.

But then only a month later, there sat Katie's room without Katie in it. Mom and I stood in the doorway peering in but unable to actually step inside. The room looked exactly as it had the last time Katie was in it.

"How will we ever go in there?" Mom asked no one in particular, more than once. "What will I do with all of her sparkly things?"

Mom walked away, but I stood there, just looking.

There was our bottle-cap collection, and her gel pens scattered everywhere, and an abandoned art project, and spilled glitter shining back at me from the floor and shelves. Her bed was still unmade from the morning the EMTs came and took her out of it and onto that gurney and away from us.

"Katie?" I whispered into the room, ridiculously.

For some reason, I remembered how before Katie died, Ms. Landers had written on one of my papers: *Jude, you have a voice, too. Use it!!!*

I opened my mouth, but nothing came out.

CHAPTER TEN

After Katie died, Gilbert came over a lot to keep me company. We played Stratego and Pokémon, and we watched television, neither of us talking very much, just sitting there occupying ourselves like usual. My parents were wrapped up in the details of Katie dying—finding a cemetery plot, planning a memorial and a burial, making a big collage of pictures of Katie happy, Katie in costumes, Katie as a baby, Katie and me, Katie with our family. They had to pick songs for the memorial and buy a tombstone and decide what clothes Katie should be buried in. I heard my mother's friend Alison say, "No mother should ever have to do this," and I agreed. But it had to get done. One day, the principal showed up with all the things from Katie's locker in a box. One day, a kid showed up with Katie's last math test and her science-project paper,

"Astrology: Science or Nonsense?" I had the bad luck of answering the door. The kid's mother hovered behind him, all twitchy like a bug, fake smiling at me and urging the kid to hand over the papers. "Thanks," I said, and I watched them both practically run to their idling car. Of course, both papers had an A+ and lots of smiley faces and exclamation marks on them.

Then, for the longest time, Gilbert didn't come over because it was Thanksgiving and then Christmas and then winter break. But even when school started again, he still didn't show up after school or on Saturdays. Sure, he played indoor soccer and also took trumpet lessons, which made him far busier than me. But I knew he was staying away because Katie was dead and that made everybody feel so awkward that even in school, at the lunch table where I'd sat practically forever with the same exact kids, no one looked at me. Oh, they talked to me and included me in jokes and stuff, but no one actually looked at me. It was kind of like I was a ghost or something. The thing was that most of them had kid sisters, and Gilbert had a sister the same age as Katie, even born the same month as Katie, and this dead-sister thing was too hard for them.

If Katie could die without any warning, then so could Violet or Sophie or Gigi. In fact, so could any of us. I guess lots of people were feeling that way.

Not one person I knew had a dead father or mother, never mind a dead sister. My world was full of healthy people, alive-and-well people, people who were going to live on and on. Of course, there were some dead grandparents and even a dead aunt or uncle. But kids and parents stayed alive. Except Katie.

But then, finally, Gilbert and his father showed up at the door one Saturday afternoon unexpectedly, as if he hadn't ghosted me all this time. Gilbert was in his soccer clothes, and his father was in jeans and a Duke sweatshirt, both looking very alive and well. I answered the door because Mom was watching her British detective show and Dad was out returning people's casserole dishes.

"Hey," Gilbert said, staring somewhere in the vicinity of my knees.

"We're on our way for pizza," his father said, "and Gilbert had the brilliant idea to invite you along. His mom and Jane are away for the weekend," he added quickly, as if seeing a normal mother with her living daughter might be too much for me. He wasn't necessarily wrong.

"Sure," I said. "I'll just tell Mom."

Gilbert and his father waited on the doorstep while I told Mom what was going on.

"This is great," Gilbert's father said when I returned, my sneakers on and a jacket in my hands. "Isn't it, Gilbert?"

We all walked to their car, and Gilbert and I got in the back and buckled up.

"Did you win?" I asked him.

"No," he said. "We suck."

It was quiet after that, except for the Sirius radio Beach Boys station playing. On the one hand, I was glad they didn't ask how Christmas break had been, because it was as sad as every week since Katie had died. On the other hand, I was kind of wishing I hadn't come. I felt like I was a pariah now, just because Katie was dead. Then I saw Gilbert's fat binders of Pokémon cards on the seat, and I pulled one out and started to play, and just like that Gilbert was playing, too, and it was like everything was all right again. I could almost hear Katie saying something like, "Pikachu! The great connector!"

At pizza, Gilbert looked straight at me and blew the wrapper off his straw right into my face. I was so happy that I laughed like a crazy person.

"What's funny?" he asked me.

"Good aim," I said, because how do you explain the way no one looks at you?

"Weirdo," Gilbert said, and he shot another wrapper at me. It hit me right on the nose.

I almost wanted to hug him, or thank him, but we weren't hugging, thanking kind of friends. Besides, how weird would it be to say, *Thank you for treating me so normally?* So I just grabbed a straw, unwrapped the tip of the wrapper, and blew. It hit Gilbert in the throat. He clutched at his neck and wiggled and rolled his eyes and gasped until his father told him enough was enough. I wished the night would never end.

Jude Banks, Superhero

I think one child is not enough, and two or three children is a good idea, but four children is too many. This family has four children, and one—a boy wearing a striped shirt that is about two sizes too small for him—looks miserable. He's probably miserable because there are too many children in his family, and for some reason he's the one nobody pays attention to. He's standing by the fence in the playground in his too-small shirt, kicking at the dirt with the toe of his sneaker. He's lucky that we're not in New Mexico, where tiny spores live in the dry dirt, and when the dirt gets blown around like that you can breathe them in and get valley fever and maybe die.

The mother is pushing one of the kids—a girl, maybe in kindergarten, with her hair in two crooked pigtails—on the swing. The other two kids—one boy, one girl—

are taking turns going up and down the curly slide, even though the boy has a cast on his hand. The cast is dirty, so I guess he broke his hand a while ago. I wonder how he broke it. Maybe he fell. Or maybe he got hit with something hard, like a fastball or a rock. Or maybe he was in a terrible accident. I wonder if he should go up and down the slide like that with a broken hand. But it doesn't seem to bother him, so I try not to worry about it.

I look back at the kid still kicking at the dirt and then the kid on the swing. Most kids who ride swings want to go higher and higher, but this one seems happy to just swing low and slow. She kind of stares off like she's thinking about something nice. The mother looks tired. Her eyes are droopy and her whole face is droopy and even her hair is droopy. Four kids makes you tired, I bet. I think about all the sandwiches she has to make every day and all the socks she has to wash and all the groceries she has to lug into the house from the car and all the times she has to say, *I said, go to sleep!* I can picture her opening the back of her minivan and lining her arms with grocery bags full of baby carrots and cherry tomatoes and whole milk and seven-grain bread and ten-for-ten-dollars worth of yogurt and boxes of cereal and hauling all of that through the garage and into the kitchen, where she has to unpack all those bags and put away all of that food.

It makes me tired just imagining it. Four kids is way too many. Two, I think, is probably perfect. One is not enough, though. Definitely not.

And then, out of nowhere, the little girl on the swing lets go of the ropes, and she's way up high, too high—I should have said something like, *Hey! Watch it! She's just a little kid!*—and what I know is that she is going to go flying off that swing and sail through the air and land on her head and get a traumatic brain injury and die, and her family will never be the same again.

I don't even bother to close my eyes. I just imagine that red cape with the sparkly purple *J* on it falling onto my shoulders, and I run toward the swings and the mother and the little girl and I am yelling, "I can save you!"

The little girl's pigtails kind of fly up and her arms open and her laughter rings through the air and I scream, "Nooooo!"

The swing has swung back down. The mother has opened her arms, and just like that, she catches her laughing, happy daughter in them. I stand there watching them, feeling like I just got kicked in the stomach because Mom will never have her daughter in her arms again. I touch my chest where my heart is and rub it as if I can somehow mend it.

Katie's Last Day

What a person would think, if a person ever thought about such a thing, is that someone's last day alive would be special somehow. I wasn't sure exactly how, but maybe she'd see an aura around everything and everyone. Or she might understand something deeply profound. Or feel a rush of pure joy, think about what a wonderful world this was, think about how much she was loved and how much she loved. She might hug the cat extra hard. She might pause to gaze at her mother's pretty face. She might look her brother straight in the eye, with such tenderness that they would both *know* that she was about to leave forever.

But no.

The last day of my sister's life was so mundane that it seemed almost unfair. Nothing special happened. She had no parting words of wisdom. She just went to bed and died.

And no one knew why. In cases like that—*sudden death,* our pediatrician, Doctor Sullivan, called it—they have to do an autopsy. According to Google, the word *autopsy* comes from the Greek *autopsia,* to see for one's self, because that's what they have to do. They have to cut up the dead person and look inside and see what happened. "Don't think about it," Dad told me when Doctor Sullivan explained that's what would happen to Katie.

Of course, all I could do was think about it. A medical examiner was going to make a Y-shaped incision from the top of each shoulder all the way down her chest, or a semicircular one, or a vertical one, or a U-shaped one, which is the kind Wikipedia says is used on women. But Katie wasn't exactly a woman yet. She didn't even wear a real bra, just a sports bra that embarrassed her. I mean, she was only eleven. They were going to use shears to open her up and they were going to take out everything, her lungs that helped her yell loud and run fast and her stomach and her big brain and her beautiful heart.

"What are you reading?" Dad asked me, maybe because he saw my look of horror or maybe because I was crying a little.

"Nothing," I said.

Doctor Sullivan told us it would take at least six weeks before we got the autopsy results. That seemed like an impossibly long time to wait.

"Can't they just tell?" Mom said.

"Not always," Doctor Sullivan said.

The next day, we got a call from the coroner telling us that a preliminary look showed a perfectly healthy eleven-year-old girl.

This made Mom so upset, she threw the phone down and screamed, "Then why is she dead, asshole?"

Seven weeks after that, the coroner called to say the autopsy results were inconclusive.

"You mean you don't know?" Mom screamed.

That was what he meant.

"I have a theory," he said. "Let me do further tests."

A million years passed, and then Dad sat me down when I got home from school and said they had the results.

"An arrhythmia. Sudden cardiac arrest," he said. "An electrical problem. Usually triggered by a loud, sudden noise."

I listened and nodded. That was a thing we used to do

when our parents explained things to us with too many words or in boring detail. "Nod and smile," Katie would whisper, and we would nod and smile while our parents droned on and on. Except now no one was smiling, and Katie was dead, so I just nodded, even though I couldn't fathom it, a loud noise stopping my sister's heart. I thought about crashing waves at Scarborough Beach. The rock music at United Skates of America. The constant screeching of our colicky cousin Amelia. All loud noises, and Katie was just fine. Death by loud noises couldn't be a real thing. It was almost too ridiculous.

"An electrical problem, Jude," Dad said again. "Like a short circuit. Like the phone rang or the coffee grinder whirred at the exact instant her heart shorted."

Or someone shouted and startled her dead, I thought, goose bumps jumping up my arms. But that couldn't be possible, could it?

"Wouldn't we know she had bad wiring?" I asked. "Because there would be signs. Symptoms. Like she'd get out of breath or faint or something."

Dad shook his head. "The first symptom is sudden death," he said sadly.

I wanted to tell him that death wasn't a symptom; it was a result, it was an end thing, a finale.

When they got the news, Mom threw away the coffee grinder, an expensive one that Dad had given her the previous Christmas because she loved her good cup of coffee so much. In its place there was just the empty spot on the counter where it had sat, so happily grinding the special beans she ordered from San Francisco for Mom's morning coffee.

"Mom didn't kill Katie," I told Dad when I saw the coffee grinder in the trash.

"No!" he said. "Of course not."

"She threw away the grinder because she thinks she did, though?"

"Look, Jude," Dad said, "Katie died before Mom even got up—"

"How can you know that?" I asked him.

"They can tell," he said quietly.

"So she died, like, in the middle of the night?" I was trying to stay calm, to not panic. I remembered how the sky looked when I went into Katie's room. It was much later than the middle of the night for sure.

Dad nodded. "It's no one's fault," he said carefully. "Mom is just looking for a reason, any reason, that something this terrible happened. The noisiest thing around was that coffee grinder. You understand that, right?"

I nodded. I maybe even said sure. But all I could think about was what had happened that night Katie died. And how I had killed her.

CHAPTER
ELEVEN

Before I turned myself in to the police, I called a lawyer who specialized in criminal cases. His name was Aaron Aaronsen, the first name to pop up when I Googled *criminal lawyers*. The picture next to his name looked like he was a bad guy in a movie—narrowed eyes, thick moustache, a certain cocked-chin pose that said, *I'm tough. Don't mess with me.* I could better imagine him beating people up than arguing in front of a judge. But tough was good, wasn't it? For lawyers?

I had to leave my name with the woman who answered the phone. She said he was in court but would get back to me as soon as possible. While I waited for him to call, I wrote down words that I could say to sound older, because what lawyer wanted to talk to a kid? *Culpable* sounded better than *guilty*, *complicated* better than *messy*.

Even though I hadn't wanted Katie to put a thesaurus on my iPad, now I was grateful.

I'd almost given up hope when Aaron Aaronsen finally did call, a gruff, "Aaronsen here," in response to my "Hello?"

"Mr. Aaronsen," I said, "my name is Jude Banks, and I find myself in a complicated situation."

"Are you a kid? You sound like a kid."

That surprised me. What kid called situations complicated?

"I think I'm culpable in a serious crime," I said, trying to make my voice deeper. "A murder."

"Seriously, kid? What'd you kill? A parakeet?"

Kid! Again!

"It wasn't intentional," I said—another big word and better than *on purpose*. "So I'm not talking about first-degree murder—"

"Second-degree murder is intentional," Aaronsen said. "It's not premeditated, but it's intentional. Like, if your parakeet wouldn't stop squawking, and you went over to your gun cabinet and pulled out your gun and shot and killed the thing, that's second-degree murder.

Getting a gun and shooting is intentional, right?"

"Uh-huh. Of course, I don't have a gun cabinet. Or a gun," I said.

"So you're talking felony murder. Not premeditated. Not intentional. Accidental, if you will. Like, if you're robbing a bank and get startled, and the gun goes off, and you shoot the bank teller. That's felony murder."

"No," I said. "That's not it. No gun."

"Okay, kid. I think you're talking about involuntary manslaughter. You're negligent, and as a result, the parakeet is dead."

"Maybe," I said.

"Do you know how much I charge for a consultation like this?" Aaronsen asked.

"A lot?"

"Consider it a gift," he said and hung up.

I ate some of the potato chips I'd started eating before he called. They were salt and vinegar, and I hated flavored chips. Where had they come from? Surely Mom wouldn't buy them. I sighed. More food from strangers.

The thing I couldn't quite figure out was if I had been negligent. I thought back to that night. How I woke up.

How I was glad the night-light was on. How I saw the light spilling from beneath Katie's bedroom door. Sometimes if we both woke up in the middle of the night, we sneaked downstairs, made microwave popcorn, and watched things on YouTube like adorable cats doing adorable things. I got out of bed, hopeful, and went to Katie's door.

Like always when I thought about that night, my brain shut down right there. I knew what I did. I *knew*. But it was like the tape broke at this instant, my hand on the doorknob, the floor cool beneath my bare feet. Then the tape jumped ahead to me back in my bed waking up to screams no kid—no person—should ever hear: the wailing grief of a mother finding her daughter dead in her bed with the tie-dyed duvet and the posters of Einstein, Shakespeare, and Mulan watching.

That day I turned myself in, I told the cop, "I think it was involuntary manslaughter." Thank you, Aaron Aaronsen. "No premeditation. No intent. No gun or anything."

Before he could say anything or slap the cuffs on me, I totally lost it. I sunk to my knees, opened my mouth, and let out something between a scream and a sob.

Doctor Botticelli
Session Six

All these afternoons with Doctor Botticelli, and he had not even once mentioned Katie. This week, he had set up a slideshow and we sat in the semidarkness, watching pictures of different places flash by on the screen: a beautiful empty beach, a rain forest, the Taj Mahal, a crowded street in London.

Each time a new picture appeared, Doctor Botticelli said something like, "You like that?" or "Would you like to go there?"

I liked all of it, sort of. Which is what I told him.

He just nodded and kept clicking the clicker to change the slide every few seconds.

After a really long time I said, "Why don't you ask me about Katie?"

From the screen, a picture of a mother-kangaroo with

a joey in her pocket looked out at us.

"Did this mama kangaroo make you think of that?" Doctor Botticelli asked me.

"I don't know. Maybe." I didn't tell him how when we were little, Katie had these red pajamas with a pouch in the front and a stuffed joey that fit inside, or how she'd put them on and hop all around the house.

He clicked the clicker, and a farm showed up on the screen.

"I just think it's weird that you never ask me anything about her," I said.

"I've been waiting until you were ready," he said.

"But that's why I came in the first place," I said.

"Jude," Doctor Botticelli said, "when you're ready, I want you to tell me what happened the night Katie died."

A big lump formed in my throat, and I found it hard to swallow. I was kind of gasping for air, trying to swallow past that lump.

Doctor Botticelli clicked the clicker, and there was a coral reef with beautiful tropical fish swimming around it.

"I'd like to go there," I managed to say.

CHAPTER

TWELVE

When we finished the poetry section in Honors English, Ms. Landers asked us to write our own poems. She said that poetry was a way to express our emotions through language and images. She used the poem "The Fish" by Elizabeth Bishop as an example.

"How does Bishop describe the fish?" she asked us.

Kids started shouting out words, like *tremendous* and *homely*.

"What simile does Bishop use to describe the fish's skin?"

Practically everybody shouted, "Wallpaper!"

Practically everybody because I didn't shout anything at all. In fact, their voices—excited and eager—made me want to scream. It was one of those feelings I couldn't explain. Not that long ago, I would have been yelling answers right along with them. Now I wanted them all to just shut up.

Ms. Landers was that kind of teacher who liked for kids to shout out things. Some teachers wanted you to raise your hand and wait to be called on. No hand raising for Ms. Landers, though. On and on she went, calling out questions about that fish, and kids shouting answers back to her, adjectives and similes falling around me. Until finally we'd gone through every moment of the relationship between Elizabeth Bishop and that fish.

"Class, at the end of this beautiful poem, the fish and the speaker connect as beings on this planet who have suffered. She has a realization when she sees those five hooks still in its mouth that it has survived near death. And what does she do?"

To my surprise, I was the only one who shouted, "Lets it go!"

Ms. Landers looked surprised, too. "Yes, Jude," she said quietly. "She lets it go."

༄

Before we left class, Ms. Landers gave us a rubric for our poem:

1. Decide which emotion you want to convey.

2. Decide what object you will use to help you convey that emotion.

3. Brainstorm adjectives to describe that object.

4. Choose a turning point. (Remember when Bishop looks into the fish's eyes, and everything becomes clear? "like the tipping of an object toward the light")

5. Outline a "plot" for your poem. (In "The Fish," Bishop catches the fish, fears the fish, recognizes the fish's struggles, and lets the fish go.)

6. Choose a last line that brings your point home. ("everything / was rainbow, rainbow, rainbow! / And I let the fish go.")

I stared at the rubric, emotionless, until Dad called me down for dinner. As I stepped out of my room, I paused at the closed door of Katie's room. The letters of her name were there, each one in a different color marching crookedly single file. I have the same colorful wooden letters spelling out JUDE on my door, but they are there more straightforwardly, a simple line of four letters smack in the middle.

"Jude!" Dad called again.

I put my hand on the doorknob and just stood there, not moving, not turning it, just standing. Like I did that night.

The morning when Mom found her, I ran out of my room and stood right there. But Dad pushed me out of the room and closed the door, telling me, "Don't come in, Jude. For God's sake, don't come in." So I didn't. I stood there and heard Mom wailing and Dad shouting into his cell phone for someone to come quickly, someone help his little girl. There were sirens and the pounding of men's footsteps up the stairs and down the hall, all of it confusing and fast and slow at the same time. "Son," one of the firemen said— Firemen? Was there a fire?—"I want you to go downstairs and sit somewhere far from all this. Okay?"

I nodded and walked downstairs to the kitchen, where everything looked completely normal: Mom's BEST MOM IN THE WORLD coffee cup sitting on the counter; apple slices on a plate on the table; two empty cereal bowls; my purple lunch box beside Katie's sparkly one, both open and awaiting our peanut butter and jelly sandwiches, our fruit and cookies; NPR on the radio.

If I sit here long enough, I thought, Katie will bound in and explain what is going on. Mom will stop that horrible wailing. The fire will be put out. And I'll eat apple slices and shredded mini wheats and go to school, hoping to not be late. But I waited and waited, and nothing ever was normal again.

There was a terrible sound of something being carried down the stairs, men saying, "Got it" and "Careful" and "There you go." The front door closed, taking with it Mom and her wailing, which were now outside and fainter but still horrible. Maybe there would be a siren. Maybe Katie needed stitches, a cast, or antibiotics.

Then the kitchen door opened, and Dad walked in, and he looked like Dad but not like Dad. He looked like all his blood had been drained from his body, like he'd grown smaller, like he'd aged a million years.

Dad looked at me, and he said, "Oh, Jude."

CHAPTER

THIRTEEN

But I didn't want to write a poem about it. I didn't even want to think about it. I used to like the way Ms. Landers kept pushing, asking why, asking how, making us think about things we'd never have thought about without her. I even liked that she wrote on my paper, *Jude, you have a voice, too. Use it!!!* But lately, Ms. Landers's digging went too deep into my broken heart, with her poems and her fish and her questions about how Elizabeth Bishop makes us all feel. How could I write about how it felt to walk around like there was a bag of stones tied around my neck? How at night even my night-light couldn't keep away the dark? How everything was dark, everything.

I Googled emotions so that I could find a different one to write about. Somewhere buried deep inside of me was a glimmer of happy. Not enough to write a poem about, but surely between grief and that slice of happy, I felt something else.

Fear. Sadness. Anger. Disgust. Surprise. Awe. Guilt. Shame. Embarrassment. Pride. Boredom. Disappointment. Contempt...

Some of the words bounced off the screen and slapped me in the face.

Fear. Anger.

Guilt. Guilt. Guilt.

I turned off my iPad and tossed it too hard onto the table. This was like a stupid City of Angels exercise. *List all the emotions you feel around the death of your sibling. Now, don't you feel better?*

If Katie were here, I'd ask for her help. I'd ask her for a metaphor for how I feel about her dying. She was good at metaphors.

One summer at a rented cottage in Truro on Cape Cod, she lay in a hammock gazing up at the bright summer sun and said, "The sun is butterscotch. The sun is a bull's-eye. The sun is white fire. The sun is a diamond."

"Huh?" I asked her in my usual brilliant way.

"Metaphors, Jude. You try."

I stared up into the sky from my own hammock, my mind as blank as a piece of printer paper.

"Go ahead," Katie said. "Try."

"The sun is a star," I mumbled.

"That's terrible!"

"Why? The sun *is* a star," I said, exasperated.

"That's why it's terrible!"

"I don't get it," I said. I opened my book and pretended to read.

"A metaphor isn't what a thing actually is. It's a metaphor," Katie said, off her hammock now and staring down at me. The sun made her red hair look like flames around her face.

I laughed. "Your hair is flames," I said, pointing at her.

"There you go!" she said, slapping me on the shoulder. "Perfect."

"Huh?" I said again.

But she was happily bouncing back to her hammock, satisfied.

꒰꒱

When Dad appeared in the doorway, I was so lost in my memory of that day that I felt confused to see him there.

"How's the homework going?" he asked.

I blinked at him.

"Need help?" he asked. "I still know an acute angle from an obtuse one. Gavrilo Princip killed Archduke Ferdinand, thus starting World War I. I even know a thing or two about rocks."

"I have to write a poem," I groaned, giving the word *poem* about a thousand syllables.

"Oh. Sorry. Not my strong point," Dad said. "Maybe Mom can help?"

I looked at him like he had just landed from Pluto. Had he noticed the shape Mom was in? Not poem-writing shape, that was for sure.

"Great. Thanks." For nothing.

"So. I'm grilling steaks," he said, as if that were normal. "For dinner," he added.

I resisted asking him who'd left a pile of raw meat on the back steps.

"How does a baked potato sound? Butter? Sour cream?"

He didn't mention bacon bits or chives, obviously. Because Katie was the one who liked them on her baked potatoes.

"Good?" I said.

He turned, to go grill the steaks, I guess. Then added a zinger: "Mom is making a salad."

"What?"

"Don't worry," he said, "no onions or anything too healthy."

Mom was actually cutting up cucumbers and tomatoes? Tearing lettuce? Making her special dressing with olive oil, lemon juice, and honey? I felt something close to happy.

I watched him walk away, but before he completely vanished around the corner he called, "City of Angels tonight?"

Maybe it wasn't so bad there. Tara texted me an inspirational saying every day, like "Tough times don't last, tough people do" and "At the end of the day, you can either focus on what's tearing you apart, or you can focus on what's holding you together." They were kind of dumb but also kind of nice. I always answered her right back— "Stay tough!" "Hold it together!"—so she knew that I read them. And the boy with acne, Mitch, also texted me a couple of times. He, too, liked inspirational quotes. I guess they were better than nothing. Then, of course, there was Clementine. She hadn't texted me, but I could maybe see her if I went.

Dad was still standing there waiting.

"Why not?" I said. "Sure."

CHAPTER
FOURTEEN

Granny was coming to visit like she did every spring, even though none of us wanted her to come. When Mom told her this might not be the best time for a visit, she said, "Nonsense! I come every spring, and I'm coming this spring." Granny was Mom's mom. She wore skirts and cardigans (her word for button-down sweaters) with brooches (her word for pins) on them and sensible shoes (her word for any shoes that were ugly and comfortable). She used to be a librarian, and she still volunteered at her local library in Concord, Massachusetts, twice a week. She made casseroles—chicken tetrazzini, tuna mushroom, shepherd's pie—and Jell-O molds in intricate shapes with fruit cocktail or canned pears suspended in them. She loved her garden and belonged to a garden club where she'd won prizes for her dahlias. Also, she belonged to a bridge club, a book club, and a movie club. Granny was always busy.

My other grandmother, Sissy, was about as opposite from Granny as two people could be. We called her Sissy because she thought Grandma or Granny or Grand-anything made her sound old, which she was. Sissy wore tracksuits in sherbet colors—raspberry, lemon, mint green—and she always had a brand-new pair of fake Nikes. She dyed her hair a color she called mahogany and had her fingernails done every week in a color she called geranium. Every morning, she met her friends at the mall, and they speed walked around it a bunch of times and then had coffee and donuts. She also played on a pickleball team. She and Pop-Pop lived in a condo that smelled like fresh paint and new carpeting, and all of their furniture was white or made of glass. The condo, Pop-Pop, and Sissy were in Arizona, where they moved when he retired. Pop-Pop mostly played golf or just stayed home and watched the History channel. Sissy also visited once a year, in summer to avoid the heat of Arizona. All summer, she and Pop-Pop visited friends and relatives who lived in places where the temperature didn't go over a hundred degrees.

When Sissy and Pop-Pop visited, they stayed at a hotel. But Granny stayed with us. She drove her 1996 Volvo from Massachusetts, with two casseroles on the floor of the back seat and her small, blue American Tourister suitcase in the trunk. She always brought us maple candy shaped like leaves, real maple syrup in a jar from her friend's maple trees, and something that we would put in the attic after she left—an old candy dish or a set of fish knives.

"I just don't want to entertain anybody," Mom said as the three of us waited on the front steps for Granny's gray Volvo to appear.

"You don't have to entertain her, Susan," Dad said, squeezing her hand. "Jude and I will pick up the slack. Right, buddy?"

"Sure," I said. I imagined I'd be playing a lot of gin rummy that weekend to *pick up the slack*.

"I just don't have the stamina for this," Mom said in a trembly voice.

I didn't think it took stamina to have Granny visit. She liked to watch *Jeopardy!* at night, read a book, play gin rummy, and talk about her dahlias. She always spent one afternoon making complicated Swedish cookies, even though she's not Swedish. It was a big deal if we could convince her to eat out at least once, whereas Sissy only wanted to eat out at Outback Steakhouse and the Hoo-Ki-Lau, the local Chinese restaurant. "There's no good Chinese food in Arizona," she'd always say, as she chowed down on egg rolls and boneless spareribs and fried rice.

"Oh dear," Mom said. "Here she comes."

Sure enough, Granny's Volvo was moving slowly down the street like a tank. When she pulled up in front of the house, she beeped twice, like she always did, even though we had already started walking toward her car.

"I just don't think I can do this," Mom said, and she wobbled a little.

Dad took her elbow and steadied her.

"Vera! You made it!" he said, with such fake enthusiasm that even Granny looked startled.

She was moving toward Mom, a tall woman dressed all in soft fawn (her word for the color of all her clothes) clothes, her arms outstretched, and Mom was standing absolutely still, crying.

It's a weird thing to say, but in that moment, I realized that Mom was somebody's child. She was Granny's child.

Even though I'd seen all the old photo albums with baby
Mom on Granny's lap and kid Mom with Granny at
Christmas and teenage Mom in a cap and gown smiling
beside Granny, I hadn't thought about Granny actually
being Mom's mother, hadn't ever thought about Granny
worrying over fevers and spills off bikes or important
decisions. I hadn't thought about how Katie dying tore
Granny apart, too.

"Oh, sweetie," Granny was saying to Mom, who had
melted into Granny's cardiganed arms and was weeping,
saying, "Oh, Mom, my Katie," and Granny kept saying,
"Oh, sweetie."

Granny's visit went exactly as it always did, except
Mom stayed in her room more than she would have if
Katie had been there. There were the Swedish cookies,
and the maple products, and lots of gin rummy. Granny's
book club was rereading Dickens, so she sat most nights
with *David Copperfield* in her hands, reading the fat book
and highlighting certain things with a blue highlighter.
We convinced her to go out one night for dinner at a
French bistro, and she would only order the French onion

soup because it was ridiculous to spend so much money on dinner.

But something very interesting did happen on Saturday night, when we got home from the French bistro. So far, no one had mentioned Katie, which was pretty typical. In general, people were afraid to even say her name. It was like she had vanished, poof! But on Saturday night, after Granny settled into a chair with her book, and Dad opened his latest *National Geographic*, and Mom started practicing her sewing, Granny said that there was something she wanted to tell us.

She had *David Copperfield* facedown in her lap, and everyone put down what they were doing and looked at her.

"It seems silly, really, to talk about this now," Granny said, "but I honestly don't know how to help this household, and for a while I've been thinking about this, what happened so long ago that I never told you, Susan. And I decided on the drive here that you should know about it."

"What? Am I not really your child or something?" Mom asked. She looked exhausted and cranky.

"Don't be silly," Granny said, and she pulled her gray cardigan closer.

"What then?" Mom insisted, even though clearly it was hard for Granny to get this story started.

"Well, when you were almost three I had another baby. A girl—"

"What?" Mom said, confused.

"Oh, it seems like a thousand years ago until I talk about it. Then it seems like yesterday. She was perfect, like you were. Rebecca. That was her name. And one day, I put her down for her nap, and when I went to check on her, she was gone."

"Kidnapped?" I blurted.

Granny looked at me, and her eyes were wet and shiny. "No, no. Gone. Dead."

The room became the kind of quiet that actually sounds noisy because everybody's breathing, and the house sounds you never usually hear all of a sudden are the only sounds.

"Only three months old, the poor little baby. They said it was crib death. But after what happened to Katie . . ."

"Oh, Vera, no," Dad was saying as he walked over to

Granny. He kneeled in front of her so they were eye to eye, the way Ms. Landers did when you were upset, and took her hands in his. "What happened to Katie wasn't genetic."

"But if I'd said something . . . Maybe you would have had her checked a long time ago? Maybe . . ." Granny looked at Mom. "We just didn't talk about things back then. There wasn't even a proper funeral. Once, I cried during bridge, and everybody got so uncomfortable I realized I had to stop carrying on."

"Mom," my mom said. "I don't even know what to say."

"There's nothing to say," Granny said. "I feel better telling you."

"Vera, really, there's no connection. What happened to your baby was something completely different."

"Well," Granny said in a way that let us know the topic was closed. She reached into the pocket of her cardigan and pulled out something. "For you, Susan," she said.

There were two photographs. One of a newborn with a wrinkled pink face, wrapped in a pink blanket. And one of a smiling kid Mom holding a baby.

Granny didn't give us any of her old stuff that weekend, like a candy dish or fish knives. Just those pictures.

Mom didn't put them in the attic or in frames. She just slipped them into her drawer after a few days of studying them.

Me, though, I couldn't stop thinking about young Granny putting her baby down for a nap and just an hour later, finding her dead in her crib. Just like Mom found Katie. Even though, as Dad said, they were different circumstances, it was still horrible in the same way. I ended up deciding that here we all are, walking through life, passing people in stores and school and restaurants, and thinking that everybody is happier or luckier than we are. But we really don't know anything about them, do we? Every single person could be holding some deep, sad secret. That idea makes me sad but also oddly comforted. I mean, I'm not the only one walking around acting normal when inside I'm crushed. Look at Granny and her dahlias. You'd think nothing bad ever happened to a woman who could grow such pretty flowers, but you'd be wrong.

CHAPTER
FIFTEEN

I was supposed to be listening to a new girl tell the incredibly sad story of her sister dying in a freak accident that involved a blow-dryer. Sitting in this circle made me want to wrap myself and everyone I loved in bubble wrap and place us somewhere impenetrable. All of these stories made the world seem unsafe, which I knew it was. I mean, Katie died in her bed, maybe the safest place anywhere except, of course, your mother's arms. I tried not to listen, tried to look like I was listening. But when I stopped listening, my mind wandered all over the place, mostly to: *Where is Clementine?* I decided to stare at the door, as if by the full force of my eyes, I could make Clementine walk in.

I narrowed my eyes and stared harder. And just like that, Clementine appeared, with her shiny hair and her mother. Why were they always late? Did they come from far away? Or were they super-disorganized people? Or did they spend too much time washing their hair? I tried to catch her eye, but she was slinking to her usual seat, eyes cast downward, shoulders slumped.

The new girl had a look about her, like she was terrified. Of life, I guessed. If your kid sister could get electrocuted blow-drying her hair, what was safe? Answer: nothing.

"The odds of someone dying from electrocution are one in twelve thousand," the girl said.

"How does that statistic make you feel?" Gloria asked. "Better? Or worse?"

The girl shrugged. "It's just interesting."

"Statistics can actually bring us comfort," Gloria said. "Knowing that only a very low percentage of people survive a certain illness, for example. Or the opposite. That the event is extremely rare and unusual."

I wondered what the statistics were for what Katie died from. Sudden death, Dad told me, is the first symptom. So I guess 100 percent died from that.

"It doesn't make me feel any better that most people *don't* die from their peanut allergy, but my sister did," Clementine said. "A food allergy sends someone to the hospital every three minutes, but usually they don't die."

Gloria nodded. "That triggers the *why-me* feeling we've talked about. If all these other people survived, why didn't *my* sister?"

Clementine scowled.

"She probably went to the emergency room—what? A dozen times? And she always came home," Gloria said.

"I don't want to talk about this," Clementine said.

"Do you want to go to the Crypt?" Gloria asked her.

"No!" Clementine shouted. "I want to go to Pluto! I want to go as far away from here as a person can possibly go! No. Wait. Pluto's not even a planet anymore."

"Neptune," I said.

Clementine glared at me. "What?"

"That's the farthest actual planet. Neptune."

Her face softened a little. Or maybe I imagined that. But she did say, "Neptune, then. I want to go to Neptune," in a softer voice.

"Me too," I said.

She even gave me a little smile then.

"Let's imagine that," Gloria said. "All of us in a rocket ship to Neptune ..."

Gloria talked us through the trip, how it would take something like twelve years to get there, and then once we arrived, we'd have to build shelter.

"Like on *Survivor*!" Tara said.

"That would be super hard," Mitch said. "It's not solid. It's all gas. When we stepped onto the surface, we'd sink."

"But eventually we'd hit the core, wouldn't we?" said Holly, the girl who smelled like Christmas trees.

I wondered why everyone knew so much about Neptune. I just knew it was the farthest from the Earth because Katie taught me *My Very Excellent Mother Just Served Us Nachos* back in fourth grade for our science test. I got one hundred on that test: Mercury, Venus, Earth, Mars, Jupiter, Saturn, Uranus, Neptune.

"Sometimes I wish I never even had a sister," Holly said.

"There's an African legend," Gloria said, and I wondered how we'd gone from Neptune to Africa so fast. "A king invites the entire village to trade their heartache for someone else's. Everybody throws their heartache into a pile, but when it comes time to choose, every single person chooses their own."

The room grew extremely quiet as the story sunk in.

If I could not have this terrible pain from losing Katie, would I take someone else's? The electrocuted sister? The brother who died of cancer? The idea of not feeling this way every minute made me think I'd take anything—anything!—else. But then I wouldn't have had Katie at all. I wouldn't have known what it was like to be her brother, to listen to her big ideas, to fall asleep holding her hand. I wouldn't trade one second with Katie for a million years of joy.

Gloria looked around the room at all of us broken kids.

"This is a good place to stop for tonight, I think," she said.

I agreed. I had the urge to run out of that room and out of that sterile office building and keep running through the cool night air, just running and running and running.

Clementine was suddenly by my side, and she was saying in a soft voice, "I almost called you yesterday, but then I chickened out."

She chickened out? She was fourteen! Her power over a twelve year old was limitless.

"The thing is," Clementine was saying, "tomorrow is Halley's birthday, and I'm practically losing my mind over it. Like, I want to yank out my heart or something."

"I don't know," I said. "Maybe we can do something special? For Halley's birthday?"

"Maybe," she said. Then she said, "She was named after the comet. Halley's Comet?"

I shook my head.

"It shows up every seventy-five years, and you can see it in the sky," she said.

"It's pretty cool to be named after a comet," I said.

"Usually Mom took us to the observatory on Halley's birthday. Mom has a thing for stars and stuff."

She looked so heartbroken standing there, so sad and lost, that I just had to cheer her up. I couldn't take her to Neptune. Or even to the observatory. But I did have an idea.

"Let's do something *super* special," I said. "To celebrate that Halley was born."

"Like what?"

"Let's skip school," I said.

Even though I had never even considered doing something like skipping school before, the idea was immediately perfect to me. No school meant no poem, at least for another day. It meant no one avoiding looking at me. It meant not having to talk about the next unit in

Earth Science: volcanoes, earthquakes, and tsunamis.

Clementine cocked her head. She was sizing me up, I could tell.

A slow smile spread across her face. "I like it, Banks," she said.

I smiled, too. I even had a nickname.

"Want to go to the cemetery?" she asked me. "The one where Halley is."

Actually, a cemetery was the last place I wanted to go.

Before I could tell her that, she added, "Heron Hills Cemetery. It's kind of nice."

"That's Katie's!"

Normal kids—and by that, I mean kids whose brothers and sisters are alive and well instead of dead—don't get excited over the same things that those of us who aren't so lucky do. For example, Clementine practically flew around the room when we discovered that our sisters were buried in the same cemetery.

"Of all the cemeteries in the world," she said, "what are the chances?"

So obviously, that was where we agreed to meet the next day.

CHAPTER
SIXTEEN

What does a person wear to meet someone at a cemetery for a dead girl's birthday party? That was what I asked myself the morning Clementine and I were meeting up at Heron Hills Cemetery. Part of me thought I should wear something special in honor of Halley. But I was supposed to be going to school, so I couldn't look *too* special. Finally, I settled on the T-shirt that Katie had tie-dyed for me a couple of summers ago when she tie-dyed practically everything, including Mom's white dinner napkins. Mom was not amused. The T-shirt wasn't special when Katie gave it to me, but it was now.

Downstairs, Mom was drinking coffee out of her WORLD'S BEST MOM mug. She looked up when I walked into the kitchen, and her face went all soft.

"The tie-dying phase," she said.

I grabbed an apple and said, "Big day today. Well, not really big, but, you know, full. A full day. Of school stuff," I added. I should have had a mug that said WORLD'S WORST LIAR.

Mom was looking at me like she knew I was up to something, so I said, "Okay, bye!" too cheerfully and headed for the front door.

But Dad appeared and said, "How about a lift?"

"No!" I practically shouted.

Dad said, "Whoa, buddy."

"Sorry," I said. Then I added ridiculously, "I need the fresh air."

"O . . . kay," Dad said.

I practically ran out of there before I could say anything else incriminating. Once I rounded the corner and wasn't on our street anymore, I slowed down. But my heart didn't, from the lying or the skipping school or because I was going to spend the day with Clementine, I wasn't sure. Probably, I decided, all three.

❧

I was not an expert on cemeteries, but I did think that this particular one, Heron Hills, was very nice. It was all rolling hills and winding paths, leafy trees and seasonal borders, like hydrangeas in summer and forsythias in fall. Former governors and mill owners and war heroes were buried there, often with large marble monuments and flags marking their graves. But there were plenty of regular people, too, and neat rows of shiny tombstones with sweet things carved into them: *loving wife, infant son, devoted mother.*

Heron Hills wasn't right on the bay but sat near enough to it that the air smelled faintly like salt water. That mixed with the scent of fresh flowers made it among the sweetest-smelling places I knew, like the bathroom after Mom took a hot shower and the air in there got filled with the smells of her cucumber soap and her fruity shampoo, or the kitchen on Sundays before Katie died and the smell of the bacon Dad fried up for breakfast lingered and mingled with whatever thing Mom was braising in the oven.

Heron Hills was so pretty, it was easy to forget that you were even in a cemetery. Entire families rode bikes along the curvy paths, joggers passed by in neon clothes, and even though a sign posted at the entrance said

No Dogs Allowed, people walked their dogs there. It was not uncommon to see a corgi or bichon pass you, its owner at the ready with a plastic bag.

Clementine and I met at the front gate, an imposing thing with ornate iron and the words *Heron Hills* decked out with copper leaves surrounding them and a copper heron subtly placed within the *N* of *Heron* and the *H* of *Hills*. I got there first, my school backpack strapped onto my back. I considered stowing it behind a tombstone, but what if it got stolen? No, I was stuck with it all day, that dumb poem I needed to write weighing me down.

Twenty minutes later, Clementine came slowly walking up the path to the gate, her shiny hair glistening in the sunlight. This was the first time I'd seen her outside the fluorescent lights of that conference room, and I noticed that her skin, like her hair, was perfect, too. She had on the same jean jacket she always wore with all kinds of buttons pinned onto it, and her high-tops with two different-colored socks—one orange and one blue-and-green striped.

"Isn't this great?" she said even before she reached me.

She spun around in a couple of lazy circles, and I saw that she did not have a backpack strapped to her back. She was, however, holding a bag with pink writing on it slung over her arm.

"I brought cake!" she said, holding up the bag.

"Great!"

"You know, for Halley's birthday," she said, right beside me now. Her eyes were as dark brown as her hair, I realized. Funny how things look so different in the sunlight.

"Nice shirt," she said.

"Katie made it," I said, surprising myself.

"I'm glad you wore it today," she said softly.

Yup, my heart was still pounding.

"I also brought paper plates and forks and cups and napkins and balloons that we need to blow up," she said. "Want to go see her now?"

"Huh?" I said in my usual intelligent way.

"Halley," she said. She pointed vaguely to the right. "She's over there."

"Oh. Okay."

The truth was, I had only been to Katie's grave twice.

And only because I had to go, not because I wanted to. There were few things worse than seeing your sister's name carved into a tombstone, even if that tombstone was pink and had a line from a Robert Frost poem on it. The dates under her name were upsetting, too—only eleven years between them, instead of ninety-six like Eli Marcum on the tombstone to the right or eighty-four and eighty-seven like Priscilla Jones, devoted wife, and Nathaniel Jones, war hero, to the left. I didn't feel like I was visiting Katie either time. I just felt miserable and like I was doing it for my parents, who wanted to plant flowers there.

"That whole fenced-off section is people who died in the Revolutionary War," Clementine said, waving her hand toward a clump of graves on a fenced-in knoll as we made our way along a path.

The tombstones were so old that some of them were half-underground with just the tops poking out. Other ones had toppled over. But some stood straight, even after all this time. I don't know why this section gave me the creeps, but it did.

She stopped walking and stared at me. "Crazy, right? These graves are like two hundred and forty years old," she added and started walking again.

"Some people like plane crashes, but for me it's war. Especially this war and these graves," Clementine continued.

"No one likes plane crashes," I said.

She stopped walking again and looked thoughtfully at me.

"Ever since Halley died, I've become fascinated by things that kill so many people without any mercy," she said. "Why do you think that is?"

I had so many ideas about why that was that I didn't know where to begin. Misery loved company? Major catastrophes could be oddly soothing when your own world collapsed? It actually felt good to know that some people out there were worse off than you were?

Luckily, Clementine didn't seem to really want an answer. She just kept going.

"This girl Nina used to come to City of Angels, and everybody wanted to be her friend because both of her brothers *and* her father had died in a plane crash. On their way to a *funeral*," she said.

"It actually feels good to know that some people out

there are worse off than you are," I said a little guiltily.

"Exactly!" Clementine said.

She motioned for me to follow her up the grassy hill to the fenced-in plot.

"Look how young some of these people were," she said softly.

I looked. James Beall was only seventeen, and his brother John—in the same plot—was only fifteen.

"I think it's better to be like James and John Beall," Clementine said. "They died on the same day. They didn't have to live with the grief."

I thought about how Mr. and Mrs. Beall must have felt, losing two kids like that. Mom had become so overprotective since Katie died because of that very fear.

Clementine had walked away by the time I looked up from that Beall brothers grave, and she was standing by what could only be Halley's grave.

Halley's tombstone had an angel on top of it, gazing skyward. It also had another name carved into it: Allan Marsh.

"My father," Clementine said. "I don't remember him. He died when I was two."

"Wow. Sorry," I mumbled.

"Yeah. Drunk driver. But honestly, I don't feel bad. I mean, I don't remember him at all."

She was fussing with a small blue trough of daisies as she talked, rearranging the flowers and centering the trough. I stared at the dates beneath Halley's name. She was my age when she died, only a year younger than Clementine, just like me and Katie.

"To me, it was always Mom and Halley and me. Girl power!" Clementine was saying. "You should have seen our house. Pink everything. And it smelled like a hair salon, we used so many hair care products between the three of us."

I almost told her she had beautiful hair but stopped myself. Besides, she had started unpacking the food, right there on her sister's grave. It was kind of early for lunch, but there wasn't really anything else to do.

"I hope you like ham and Swiss, because that's all we had," she said, taking out two sandwiches wrapped in plastic wrap.

I glanced around. "Shouldn't we maybe eat over there? On that bench?" I pointed to an ornate iron bench nearby.

Clementine laughed. "That's where Mary Margaret Madison has her ashes buried," she said. "*Sit. Feast on your life.* That's what the plaque says. Apparently it's a quote from some poem by Derek Walcott? That's what Mom said."

"Where are her ashes buried, exactly?"

"Under the bench. Apparently her dream was for sad people to sit there and contemplate life or something. Also what Mom said."

She took a big bite out of a sandwich. "When we're done, we can go to Katie's and hang out. It makes me feel better, being here. Don't you feel better?"

"Uh-huh," I said, though I did not feel better being there. I did, however, feel better being with Clementine. And not just because she was so pretty and shiny, but because she understood. I didn't have to explain anything about how I felt—she knew because she felt the same way. Who else would be able to say that she envied an entire family who'd died of the Spanish influenza without worrying about sounding crazy?

❧

I didn't want to admit that I never came to the

cemetery or that I wasn't even sure where Katie's grave was, but luckily we hadn't walked very far when I recognized the obelisk with a dead governor's name on it. That day at the funeral, when I wanted to look away from my mother's tortured face or the white coffin topped with pink flowers, I'd stared at that dumb obelisk.

"Right down here," I said, leading the way, past the obelisk a few rows.

Sure enough, there it was. Pink granite. Katie's name. *Wing to wing, oar to oar.*

"What's that mean?" Clementine said.

"It's from a poem."

"Funny how many people put poetry on their tombstones," she said. "I don't want poetry on mine. Just the basics. When people walk by, I want them to gasp and say, *Oh! She died so young!*"

"If you die young," I said.

"I will," she said.

She knelt down and pressed her cheek to the stone. "Hi, Katie," she whispered.

"But you don't know that," I said. "That's one of the things that drives me crazy. We don't have a clue when we—or anyone—is going to die. Katie had a perfectly normal day that day."

"Well," Clementine said, "I know I'm going to die young. You know, you need to get some flowers or something. It's so empty here."

"My mom takes care of that."

"Well, apparently not. There's nothing here."

I realized I was staring at the obelisk.

"It's so obnoxious," Clementine said. "That giant thing, like he's more important than Halley or Katie or anyone."

I shrugged. "He was the governor."

"One stupid term! In 1904!"

"Do you know every single grave in here?"

"I'm a very curious person," she said.

❧

I admit it was weird, but we spent the rest of the time visiting Clementine's favorite graves. The one with three children who all died on a different Christmas day. The one written in another alphabet. The one that described the guy as a seafarer and a gentleman. The one with the family dog also buried there. On and on we walked, taking turns reading inscriptions out loud. I liked the old-fashioned names—Jebediah and Patience and Ephraim. She liked the most tragic, the lists of dead children, the ones that just said *Infant Daughter*.

Walking home alone, I realized I felt better than I'd felt in a long time. Until my phone buzzed in my pocket, and I took it out and read the text from Clementine: "I killed my sister," it said.

Without even pausing, I typed: "So did I."

And hit SEND.

Jude Banks, Superhero

Did you know it only takes forty-five seconds for a kid to drown in a pool? That's why I'm staying so close to this little kid, Dylan. No one is really paying attention to him, and he's spinning in circles on the wet pool pavement, trying to make himself dizzy the way little kids do, and he could spin himself right into the water and no one would even notice. Except me.

His mother is throwing this indoor pool party for his older brother's birthday, and she invited the whole neighborhood. I didn't want to come because who wants to go to a seven year old's birthday party? Also, I have not been in a celebration mood since Katie died. I didn't even go to Gilbert's bowling party last month. But Mom insisted. Her grief counselor told her she should do one thing a week she doesn't want to do, and lucky me, I get to do it with her.

Every now and then, Dylan's mother looks away from her margarita and her conversation until she spots him. She gives him a wave or a thumbs-up, and then she goes right back to talking about things that don't matter. His father is outside at the grill with the other fathers, a beer bottle in his hand and his back turned away from the pool. When I went out there, he was giving advice on what to do with the hamburgers. There's a debate going on over by the grill: Is it better to leave the burgers alone or to flatten them with the spatula? Dylan's father is on the side of leaving them alone. All this while his kid spins in circles, getting dizzier and dizzier, right by the edge of the deep end.

But I'm ready to save him. I'm standing close by, and if he slips into the water, I will jump in right after him in one, two seconds, at the most. I will be a hero. Standing there, I feel powerful. No, superpowerful. I can practically hear my superhero cape flapping ever so slightly in the breeze.

Out of nowhere, Dylan spins crazily toward me and drops right at my feet. He has those weird water wings on his arms and a bathing suit covered in neon surfboards.

"Hey, you," he says in his little-kid voice. "Get away from me."

"I'm here to save you," I tell him softly.

And in a nanosecond, his face contorts into a howling mask and his mouth opens wide and all his tiny teeth are showing and he's screaming for his mother, who races over and scoops him up into her sunburned arms.

"What happened?" she demands, staring at me like I'm to blame.

"I was just standing here," I say. I sound weak and timid, not at all like a superhero.

"He's creepy!" Dylan screams. "He's following me!"

I see my mother's face, bleary from margaritas, turned toward me from her chaise lounge alone in the corner. She seems confused. I can tell she's trying to decide if she should come over or wait it out. Telepathically, I send her a message: *Stay there.* Maybe she receives it, because she slowly looks away again and pulls her sunglasses, which were perched on her head, back over her eyes.

Brainstorming:
Ms. Landers, Poetry Unit

Grief is a stone in your stomach, a stone on your back,

 a stone in your heart.

Grief is gray, black, violent red.

Grief is a storm at sea, a tsunami, a meteor.

Grief is like arrows piercing you. Grief is like a nuclear

 bomb. Grief is every war combined. It's the black

 death, the 1906 San Francisco earthquake, 9/11,

 all rolled into one and aimed just at you.

Grief is a canyon, a crevasse, a black hole.

Grief is shards of glass. Grief is flayed skin. Grief is leprosy.

Grief is a scream.

Grief is endless, like the horizon or pi or space.

CHAPTER
SEVENTEEN

Mom started to make a quilt out of Katie's clothes. I found this to be the saddest thing of all the sad things that had happened lately—the pathetic dinners on our doorstep, the British detective show, the staring. For one thing, my mother didn't know how to sew. She tried to teach herself, but it didn't go very well. For another thing, I couldn't bear the sight of Katie's clothes strewn everywhere, on chairs and tables and the living-room rug. Mom said she needed to get a sense of patterns and color combinations. But those clothes—her striped and polka-dot and crazy-colored twirly skirts, her sparkly T-shirts, her faded blue jeans and the weird holiday shirts she liked with smiling pumpkins or elves on them—they just reminded me of how Katie wasn't here anymore.

At first, Mom watched YouTube videos. "Come watch,

Jude!" she said enthusiastically. So I went and sat with her on the couch, her computer propped up on her knees. The first person talked about a walking foot. "Uh-oh," Mom said and clicked on the next video. "Let's talk about basting for a minute," the woman said, and Mom clicked again. The next woman said she was excited about tube quilting. "But could it be done with a regular ruler?"

"Do you know what this means, Jude?" Mom said, looking defeated. She didn't wait for me to answer. "It means I have to actually go and take sewing lessons somewhere."

Next thing I knew, she'd enrolled in a quilting class at Forget-Me-Knot, a craft store that she used to make fun of. *Look at all those people in there, crocheting afghans no one wants!* she'd say, even though she had been knitting Katie and me those blankets forever. *That's different*, she told me, but I wasn't sure how. All of a sudden, she couldn't wait to go to Forget-Me-Knot and learn to make a quilt.

On Saturday mornings, she took Basic Sewing with Amanda Jones, who was also my school's librarian. I found this embarrassing, my mother learning how to thread a needle and sew hems with the same person who suggested books to me for my book reports. Then, on Monday nights, she took Beginners Quilting. That was taught by Mrs. Pidgeon, the oldest woman in the world. Or so it seemed to me. Hunchbacked, balding, nearsighted, Mrs. Pidgeon looked like she came straight out of a fairy tale. She smelled like a combination of mothballs and wet wool. How did I know this? I had to sit in Forget-Me-Knot on Mondays while Mom took her Beginners Quilting class because Dad had started taking a class of his own at the junior college: the Art of Collage. And I wasn't allowed to sit in the classroom because of liability issues.

Since my parents wouldn't leave me at home alone, I was forced to sit in the corner of Forget-Me-Knot while a bunch of women cut shapes out of fabric and discussed things like batting, piecing, and bias tape. My parents used to leave Katie and me alone, mostly on Saturday nights so they could go to a dinner party or a movie. *Even old people like us need a date from time to time!* Mom would put on perfume and lipstick, and Dad would wear his nice loafers, the ones with tassels. But now they wouldn't hear of me staying home by myself. What if I fell? What if the house caught fire? What if someone broke in? In other words, what if I died, too?

In between Beginners Quilting and Basic Sewing, Mom arranged and rearranged Katie's clothes.

"How does this look side by side?" she'd ask me, and she'd hold up a pale-blue shirt and a navy-blue twirly skirt covered with shooting stars.

It looked like the day Katie won the spelling bee last year. The winning word was *connoisseur*, and I could tell by the huge smile that lit up Katie's face when Ms. Landers said it that she knew how to spell it. I had gotten eliminated two rounds earlier with the word *Seoul*, as in the capital of South Korea (I knew this only because that was the definition Ms. Landers gave me). But Katie had successfully spelled *satiate* and *salvageable* to make it to the final round with Violet Cyrhh and Alexandra Vance. Violet and Alexandra did not smile when Ms. Landers said *connoisseur*.

"Or do you like this better?" Mom said. She shoved Katie's Pepto-Bismol-pink jumper and crazy striped long-john shirt in my face.

That was the day Katie sprained her ankle trying to break the Guinness World Record for jumping jacks, which was 103 in one minute by Kapil Kumar in India.

Katie only got to fifty-seven before her feet got tangled up and she tripped, spraining her ankle.

"I hate quilts," I said softly.

Mom frowned. "Nobody hates quilts, Jude. They're beautiful. Did you hear Mrs. Pidgeon tell us that some people believe African American slaves used a quilt code to navigate the Underground Railroad? She said that there were quilts with patterns that contained secret messages about it."

Mom took out her quilting scissors, weirdly shaped things with purple handles, and cut Katie's Pepto-Bismol jumper in half, right up the seam.

I couldn't bear to watch. I wanted to scoop up all of Katie's clothes and run out the door with them to save them. Maybe I could hide a secret message in their patterns: Katie, Come Home.

Text Messages from Clementine

Do you ever wish you could really go to Neptune, Banks?

Not a fan of planets that glow blue.

How about just disappearing?

Better.

I think about it all the time.

CHAPTER
EIGHTEEN

Tonight at Forget-Me-Knot, Mrs. Pidgeon was discussing, in excruciating detail, the various quilt patterns, when Clementine and her mother walked in.

It was kind of like a bad dream: I was sitting way in the corner, in a worn-out armchair where I could feel the springs poking my butt, trying to write my stupid poem, which in just the twenty minutes I'd been sitting there had the titles "Black Hole, Stormy Sea, Tsunami," and "Shards of Glass," the last one too reminiscent of *Leaves of Grass* by Walt Whitman, but hey! I was desperate, and Mrs. Pidgeon was saying things like "Log Cabin" and "Tumbling Blocks" and "Hunter's Star" while flashing pictures on the wall with some kind of machine that was about as old as she was. "Log Cabin," she'd say in her old, crackly voice, then there'd be a *click* and a picture of a quilt would appear on the wall next to the button display.

Mom was taking careful notes, and I was writing down words that kind of rhymed with *tsunami* since the only word that rhymed with *glass* that I could think of was *ass*. So far, under my crossed-out titles, I had: *pastrami, salami, zombie (?), Mommy*. The door opened, and in walked Clementine and her mother. I slumped down in my chair because I did not want to be seen at number one, Forget-Me-Knot, and number two, a quilting bee. Hadn't Clementine asked me if I'd like to disappear? Yes, yes, yes!

"Flying Geese," Mrs. Pidgeon intoned with a click, and a picture of a quilt with brightly colored triangles appeared on the wall. Every quilt, it seemed to me, was made of triangles.

"We need more of the Dreambaby DK Paintpot in Rosebud," Clementine's mother said in a stage whisper to the woman who sat knitting by the cash register during Beginners Quilting.

"Jude?" Clementine said in a way-too-loud voice.

I swear every head turned toward me, even Mrs. Pidgeon's ancient one.

Clementine marched over to me, with a sort of smile

on her face. "Don't tell me you knit," she said.

I slumped down lower and shook my head.

"Because when Gloria sent that email suggesting we learn a craft, like knitting, because it calms the voices in our head, Mom and I said, why not? I didn't know you were doing it, too."

Now I got it. That was why all of a sudden my father was taking the Art of Collage and my mother was taking Basic Sewing and Beginners Quilting, and one of them had left a brochure on my bedside table for something called Crafts for Kids with a class for Creating Woodland Animals circled in green Sharpie.

"So we're making baby hats for preemies," Clementine said. "It's so boring."

"Preemies?"

"Premature babies," she said. "Some only weigh, like, a pound, and they have to live in incubators, and they can't even have their mothers hold them."

"Why do they need hats if they live in incubators?" I asked.

"Apparently their heads are super cold," Clementine said. "Maybe because they're so small?"

"Clementine?" her mother called in that stage whisper. "I got some sherbet and daisy, too." She held up some balls of yarn in various shades of pink.

Clementine took stock of the room.

"Honeycomb," Mrs. Pidgeon said and clicked.

"Wait. You don't knit. You're . . . quilting?" she said. "That's so . . . like, *Little House on the Prairie*."

"No!" I said loud enough for my mother to frown at me over her notebook.

I cleared my throat. "Actually, I'm going to start to make woodland animals."

"What does that mean?" Clementine said, looking baffled.

"You know, like chipmunks."

"Make them out of what?"

Luckily, her mother motioned for her just before I offered *fur* because I had no idea what the whole woodland-animal thing was about.

Clementine leaned over, her fruity-smelling hair falling into my face, and whispered, "If you want to cut school again—"

The weight of my poem—*pastrami, salami, Mommy*—

felt as heavy as, well, stones.

I didn't want to write that poem. I didn't want to expose my grief to the whole class. But the principal had called the day Clementine and I skipped school, and Mom had walked into my room frowning and said, "Jude? You weren't in school today?"

And I'd held up the poem-brainstorming paper and said, "Huh? Where do you think I got this?"

"Oh, Jude," Mom had said, "please don't start doing things like skipping school."

So I even surprised myself when I heard myself whisper, "Tomorrow?"

She took a step back and smiled. "I like the way you think, Banks," she said. "Tomorrow."

"Clementine?" her mother said.

"Broken Dishes," Mrs. Pidgeon said. *Click!*

Clementine walked away with a toss of her hair, leaving a faint smell of strawberries behind.

Mom was still frowning at me, or frowning at me again. I picked up my pen and wrote *balmy, commie, origami.* Maybe a poem was starting to take shape.

Things I Would Tell You about Katie

I knew Katie since she was born. Dad brought me to the hospital to see her when she was only two hours old, and we have a picture of me, practically a baby myself, at eleven months old, dressed all in blue and holding her in my lap with Dad's arms around mine really doing the holding. In the picture, her hair is already the orangey red it would be for her whole life.

"Do you know how special redheads are?" she'd ask me years later, when we were in third grade. "Only two percent of the entire population of the world has red hair!"

"Do you know how special redheads are?" she'd ask me the next year, in fourth grade. "We only have ninety thousand strands of hair, while people like you have one hundred and forty thousand strands!" I thought that made people like me—with brown hair, I guessed—

more special. I mean, we had more strands than anyone else! But by then, I'd learned not to argue with Katie when she was trying to make a point.

"Do you know how special redheads are?" This was in fifth grade. "There are actual festivals celebrating us! All over the world! Like, Russia and the Netherlands and Ireland!"

She paused to come up for air, then: "We should have a festival here! Will you be on the committee?"

Luckily, the next year she did her final report on how special redheads were, so she didn't have to talk about it endlessly anymore.

"People in the Bible with red hair include King David, Mary Magdalene, and Judas Iscariot. In Norse mythology, Thor was a redhead," she said in her oral presentation, which also included the Middle Ages, Ayurveda, Western beliefs, genetics, and that redheads need a higher dose of anesthetics before surgery.

"Very thorough!" our teacher said when Katie, finally, sat down.

That was Katie. Thorough.

Tsunami

BY JUDE BANKS

I was walking on the sunlit beach
Blue skies, laughing children,
You right there, within my reach,
When out of nowhere—
No deafening roar or rumbling earth—
A wave rose high right there
As I watched.
Tsunami, you came and washed away
The thing I held most dear.
Tsunami, your destruction
Is more than I can bear.

CHAPTER
NINETEEN

I woke up to the sound of rain falling hard on the roof above my room and across the windows, leaving wet slash marks.

My first thought: Get Katie, put on wellies, run outside and jump in puddles.

My second thought: Katie is dead.

I put a pillow over my head and squeezed out the tears that had filled my eyes right along with that second thought.

Third thought: Clementine. We couldn't meet up in this weather.

A knock on my door, followed by Dad calling to me to wake up. "I'll give you a lift to school," he said. "But you'll have to get a move on."

I grunted at him. As soon as his footsteps disappeared,

I sat up and wiped my wet cheeks with the back of my hand, then reached for my phone to text Clementine. But she'd already texted me, hours earlier.

> Too depressed to meet. Sorry.

> It looks like even the sky is crying today.

I guessed I had poetry on the brain. While I waited for her to respond, I tried to remember what it was called when you said things like "the sky is crying." Pathetic fallacy? I actually started to get off the bed to go ask Katie, who knew about everything from onomatopoeia to allusion and beyond. Last year, she challenged me to only talk in onomatopoeia for an entire afternoon, the two of us walking around saying *bang* and *plop* and *rat-a-tat-tat*.

Next thought: Katie's dead.

No reply from Clementine, so I slid back under the covers and put the pillow back over my face. This was not a good day.

After six months and Katie staying dead, things had settled into good days and bad days, which was much better than how they'd been—all bad days. When Mom had a bad day, she watched her British detective show and didn't eat dinner and either cried nonstop or stared at nothing like a crazy person. When she had a good day, she cut Katie's clothes into triangles or made huge vats of stuff like chicken stock or spaghetti sauce that she lined up in the freezer in mason jars. Sometimes when she had a good day, she'd suggest we all go for a drive or a walk or to a movie. That almost felt normal, sitting in a dark movie theater sharing a jumbo popcorn, extra butter, with Mom. Katie and Dad liked theirs with no butter, so they always shared. These days, Dad doesn't get popcorn at all.

When Dad had a bad day, he hid behind a book. It was almost like the book was a shield between him and everything else. Dad liked big books about people like John Adams or historical events. He could hide behind those books for a long time. On bad days, he also did chores that didn't really need to be done. He'd wash the cars, inside and out. He'd move plants around the garden or order seeds from the Burpee catalog. He'd vacuum under the beds or check the carbon monoxide detector. On good days, he just acted like Dad.

I had good days when I hung out with Gilbert at his house. We'd play Pokémon or Stratego, and his mom would make chocolate-chip cookies for us, and sitting in his kitchen, with its yellow curtains and wind chimes made out of old forks and spoons, everything seemed pretty normal. Isn't is weird that a house that didn't have a kid die looks pretty much the same, and a house that did have a kid die—ours—looked completely different? Mom didn't rearrange the furniture or paint the walls or anything, but somehow the house without Katie looked completely different. His family had all kinds of things that moved—scooters, bikes, Rollerblades, you name it—as well as every kind of ball—soccer, tennis, football, everything—and after we ate the cookies and drank the weird organic milk his mother bought, she'd make us go outside for fresh air, and we'd race up and down his long driveway on something with wheels or throw balls at each other, and it was the only time that I felt stuff was actually okay.

When I had a bad day, I forgot that Katie had died. And then I'd remember, and it felt almost as bad as when it had happened. Like a kick in the stomach or a giant invisible hand reaching into my chest and squeezing my heart hard. Nothing seemed right for the rest of the day after that. Instead, everything was a reminder of no Katie: no Katie in school, no Katie in her bedroom, no Katie in this whole wide world.

That was how I felt that rainy day. It was a bad no-Katie day, right from the start. The ride to school with Dad was sad and quiet, and I had the feeling that if he could pick up the John Adams biography right then, he would have, even though he was driving. When we got to school, Dad reached across the seat and pulled me into a big hug, the kind of hug that feels like the person might never let you go. Maybe rain made everyone sad? The sky was so gray, and the rain was so relentless, a person couldn't help but feel hopeless.

In Earth Science, we learned that most people who died in earthquakes died from the fires that followed, not from falling buildings. In Math, we added and subtracted negative numbers. In Social Studies, we started a new unit on Lewis and Clark, and Henry had to go stand in the hallway because he couldn't stop laughing about Lewis's name being Meriwether Lewis. Even after class, Henry kept asking everybody, "Doesn't Meriwether sound like a girl's name?" Everybody pretty much ignored him. Lunch was pizza that tasted like cardboard with a side of wrinkly peas, and by the time it was over, I wished that I was anywhere but there, maybe in the cemetery with Clementine or even back in my bed with a pillow over my face.

And the whole day it just rained and rained. We couldn't go outside when it rained, so the art teacher, Mrs. Kukk, took us to the gym and taught us Estonian folk dances. While we all held hands and danced around in a circle, I kept eyeing the emergency exit and debating whether I could get away unnoticed. On one side, I had to hold Sophie's sweaty hand, and on the other side, I had to hold Emma's fingers because she had a cast and only her fingers were holdable.

Just when I thought I'd be stuck dancing in a circle forever, the bell rang, and Mrs. Kukk said we did great and taught us to say "hüvasti," which is goodbye in Estonian. On my way to Honors English, I debated going to the nurse and pretending I had a stomachache. She had a small cot in her office, and if you had a stomachache she gave you ginger ale and let you lie there until you felt better or a parent came and took you home. The idea of it was so nice, the scratchy blanket on that cot, and the warm ginger ale, and Nurse Barb restocking her supply of Band-Aids while you closed your eyes. But then Nurse Barb would call Mom, and what if Mom was also having a bad day? What if she came to get me wearing her pajamas? Or what if she didn't come at all?

That was how I found myself in Honors English class with Ms. Landers announcing, "Today we are going to peer edit our poems!" like this was the most fun we'd ever have in our entire lives.

She told us about the importance of editing and how even our favorite writers, like John Green and Louisa May Alcott, had their work edited.

"Did Meriwether Lewis have his work edited?" Henry blurted, then set off laughing again.

"Knock it off already!" Justin Burr shouted. There was a rumor that he was a distant relative of Aaron Burr, the guy who killed Alexander Hamilton in a duel. That added to Justin's already menacing personality.

Ms. Landers frowned and reminded Henry that Meriwether Lewis was an explorer, not a poet, and she told

Justin to keep his opinions to himself. Then she assigned our peer editors, and my bad day got even worse because my peer editor was Ava Morton-Wicke, know-it-all, mean girl, enemy to Katie, and all-around worst person in the entire world.

"Please take fifteen minutes to read your partner's poem. You'll then have fifteen minutes to discuss your poems with each other and share your editing comments," Ms. Landers said.

Everybody shifted seats so that we were facing our partners. Ava had a ponytail and daisy earrings. Was it a coincidence that her poem was titled "Fields of Daisies"? I thought not.

Mostly I just stared at her dumb poem, which was a sonnet (she pointed this out to me when she slid the poem across my desk: *See? Fourteen lines with the AB, AB rhyme scheme and the couplet at the end?*) about love. What did a twelve year old know about love, anyway? Ava and Aiden MacDonald "went out," a euphemism (thank you for that word, Katie!) for them sitting together at lunch and going to each other's sporting events. *But do not pluck a daisy before its time, Or hearts will break and poems not rhyme.*

That was the couplet at the end. When Ms. Landers announced that it was time to discuss with our partners, I had absolutely nothing to say. I mean, who would pick a daisy before it bloomed? You'd just have a stem, right?

"Jude," Ava said in a deeply somber voice, "this poem is about Katie, isn't it?"

"Sort of," I said. "It's about, you know, grief."

Ava nodded. "The tsunami," she said.

She wiped at the corners of her eyes.

"I miss her so much," Ava said, sounding like she was on the verge of crying.

"But you weren't even friends," I reminded her.

Her eyes widened. "Don't you remember at my birthday party in second grade when I had the animal guy come, and I let her hold the hedgehog first?"

"No."

"And in September, right before she, you know, passed away, I told her how much I liked her outline on the history of musical theatre." Ava leaned closer. "I was her peer editor for that. I'll never forget how good that outline was."

I had an overwhelming urge to punch Ava Morton-Wicke right in her face. Or to yank her ponytail out, or throw her stupid daisy poem out the window.

"I . . . I have to go," I said, and I rushed out of class, straight to Nurse Barb.

"I want to go home," I told her. "I have a stomachache."

"Oh, Jude," Nurse Barb said. "Lie down, and I'll get you some ginger ale."

Since it was last period, she didn't even have to call my mother. I could just close my eyes and clutch my stomach, pretending it hurt, until the bell rang and it was time to go home.

I practically ran the whole way through the rain that was falling as if it might never stop. I didn't have on my wellies because Dad drove me, so my sneakers were drenched and my whole self was drenched by the time I walked into the kitchen, dripping onto the floor. I was surprised to see both Mom and Dad sitting there, looking worried.

"Why aren't you at work?" I asked Dad as I began to peel off my wet sneakers and socks.

They both stood up at the same time.

"Why are you guys acting so weird?" I said. I was barefoot, and the fake Italian floor tiles felt cold and hard beneath my feet.

"Your friend from City of Angels," Dad began.

"Tara?" I said, suddenly afraid. Tara had texted me an inspirational quote that morning and I hadn't answered her.

"No, not Tara—"

"Clementine?"

They both nodded.

"Buddy, she did something really dumb. She swallowed a whole bottle of Advil and she's in the hospital," Dad said.

"Why did she do that?" I asked, not getting it.

Mom and Dad looked at each other.

"She left a note," Dad said. "Tell Jude I've gone to Neptune. Tell him I'm sorry," he recited.

I let his words sink in.

"You mean," I started, but I couldn't say the words out loud.

Mom wrapped me in one of those hugs that seem like they'll never end.

"She tried to kill herself," Dad said.

I was crying into Mom's bony shoulder, crying and hoping that she'd never let me go.

Texts I Wrote but Did Not Send To Clementine

You are not allowed to die.

Advil??? Really???

Please don't ever do anything remotely like this again. Please.

How could you? Just when we were becoming friends? I am so mad at you I could throttle you!

I hate you.

You didn't know this, but I have a doppelganger who is a superhero and saves lives. He's British. And brave. And he will be watching you.

The Text I Did Send To Clementine That She Did Not Answer

I know how sad you feel. But so many people care about you and would be devastated if anything happened to you. Like your mom. And me. Are you out of the hospital? Did they pump your stomach like on Grey's Anatomy? Can I visit you?

Emergency Session with Doctor Botticelli

For once, Doctor Botticelli didn't make me look at art or listen to music or choose my favorite flower. Instead, as soon as I sat down and blurted out what had happened, he said, "Wow. This is pretty terrible, isn't it?"

And I said, "Yes, it is."

We sat in the quiet for quite some time before Doctor Botticelli said, "Advil doesn't usually kill you."

"I'm not sure."

"What I mean is, I think your friend, Clementine, just wanted her parents to notice how much pain she was in. She did something impulsive and dramatic that I bet she wishes she could take back."

"I don't think so," I said. "She's been talking about going to Neptune, and I should have realized she wasn't being metaphorical."

"How could you have realized that?"

"By paying attention better."

We were quiet again. That noisy kind of quiet. Every now and then, I heard a buzzer buzz, someone at the front door for an appointment. Doctor Botticelli's office was in an old Victorian house with steep steps and offices where bedrooms used to be when people lived here. The whole place was full of psychologists, so if you passed someone coming in or going out they always looked slightly embarrassed, like you'd caught them doing something wrong. There was also the hum of the dehumidifier he had going in the corner. It hummed for a long time and then paused ever so briefly before it started humming again.

As if he knew what I was thinking, Doctor Botticelli said, "It's so damp in this old house that I need that thing on all the time."

"She only has a mother," I said.

He leaned forward slightly.

"Her father died a long time ago."

"Do you really think she'd do something that would cause her mother more pain, then?" he said, wisely I thought.

"Good point," I conceded.

"She's in so much pain, and she needs people to notice. To understand. So she did this very dramatic act to show everyone her pain," he said.

I nodded because that did make sense.

"Also, she thinks she's responsible for what happened to Halley. Her sister," I said.

"How so?"

"I'm not sure. Halley died of a peanut allergy."

Now Doctor Botticelli leaned back. "What do you think about her feeling guilty?" he said.

I guessed that was my opportunity to confess my own guilty feelings, to tell Doctor Botticelli what I'd done the night Katie died. But the words weren't words yet. They were just one big awful feeling that didn't have shape or order to it.

So instead we just sat there until Doctor Botticelli asked me if I felt any better, and I said yes and left.

CHAPTER TWENTY

Gloria looked at us sitting in the circle and said, in a serious voice that made everyone stop whispering and fidgeting, "Something very, very disturbing has happened to one of us." It was the first time I could remember that she wasn't wearing her hat. She had lots of dark curls, like a waterfall of curls.

I wanted to run out of that room as fast as I could. I didn't want to hear the words. Something about hearing a thing said out loud made it even worse. *Buddy, I am so sorry to have to tell you this, but Katie died.*

"Clementine Marsh attempted suicide a few days ago," Gloria said.

A gasp swept through the room. Someone said, "No!" in a long, low moan.

"It was her sister's, Halley's, birthday last week,"

Gloria said, "and milestones like that can really set us back."

A few people were crying. I thought about us at Heron Hills on Halley's birthday, how Clementine didn't seem at all like a person who was going to swallow a bottle of Advil. She just seemed sad, like all of us in this room.

"I understand how deep that pain runs. I understand that disappearing forever seems like a solution. But, guys, it isn't. Do you think your sister or brother would want you to do that?" Gloria said, her eyes seeming to pause on each one of us. "Do you think your parents could take more grief?"

"Did she, like, cut her wrists?" Tara asked.

"I think that's irrelevant," Gloria said.

"I was just wondering," Tara said.

I gave Tara the stink eye, but she ignored me.

"That isn't the answer to what you're feeling," Gloria said. "The answer is to move through it to the other side. You don't walk around the valley of the shadow, you walk through it."

"The what?" someone asked.

"It's from the Bible," Gloria said. "Now, you know I'm not here to force any particular religion on you, okay?

But I do think the twenty-third psalm speaks to those of us grieving. It tells us, 'Though I walk *through* the valley of the shadow of death, I will fear no evil. Thy rod and thy staff, they comfort me. You prepare a table before me in the presence of my enemies. You anoint my head with oil, my cup overflows. Surely goodness and mercy shall follow me all the days of my life."

We all sat quietly, maybe thinking about the twenty-third psalm, maybe wondering how Clementine tried to kill herself, maybe just waiting for the pizza. But I think because we were studying a poetry unit at school, those words did have meaning for me. They said that someone cared about you, no matter what. That your cup overflows.

"Jude?" Gloria said. "I think you've responded to it, haven't you?"

"I don't know," I mumbled.

"Really? Because I got the impression—"

"Well, I don't know. It tells us that our cup overflows, that goodness and mercy will stay with us forever."

"And that makes you feel what?" Gloria prodded.

It felt like everyone in that circle was staring at me.

I could feel their eyes boring into me, right through my flesh and bones.

"Jude?" Gloria said.

"I don't know. Hope?" I said.

"Yes," Gloria said, nodding. "Hope."

"It's kind of hard to feel hope when your mother cries all day, your father is hardly home, and you and your brothers are heating up canned soup every night for dinner," Mitch said. "It feels pretty bleak."

"I know," Gloria said. "But the thirteenth-century Sufi mystic Rumi said, 'Grief can be the garden of compassion. If you keep your heart open through everything, your pain can become your greatest ally in your life's search for love and wisdom.'"

She looked around again in that way she had of making eye contact with every one of us.

"Your greatest ally," she repeated. "Think about that."

We grew quiet, though I'm not sure who was actually thinking about that. Even though that psalm made sense to me, and even though Ms. Landers kept telling us that poetry could heal us, unite us, and comfort us, it did just feel like a bunch of words. Because even after I thought about grief being my ally and keeping my heart open and how I had to walk *through* the valley of the shadow of death and not around it, in the end Katie was still dead. I could read or write a million poems, and that fact would never change.

Jude Banks, Superhero

I'm in the library, not the school library but the real library, the big stone library with a million steps leading up to the front door with the owl carved above it. Every time I climb those stairs and see that owl, I can practically hear Katie talking to me, all excited.

"It's the owl of Athena, Judester!"

"Greek goddess of wisdom," I said. We loved Greek mythology. One of our favorite things to do one summer was dress up in sheets and act out myths.

"There's the little owl that always accompanies her," Katie said.

I nodded. That was why owls represented knowledge.

"Hi, little owl," I whisper this afternoon, glancing up at it. The slightest breeze passes by, and for an instant, I let myself believe it's Katie patting me on the back.

Inside, the library smells like old books and coffee. A couple of years ago, the town added a café where the children's section used to be, right by the reference desk. Mom said it was to bring more people into the library, but mostly people who have nowhere else to go sit in the café and read the free newspapers and magazines. But Katie used to like to go there with a stack of books and learn new things.

"Trench foot!" she'd say in horror, holding up a book about World War I and pointing to a black-and-white photograph of a rotting foot, possibly with a few toes missing.

"The bee hummingbird!" She showed me a picture from an Audubon Society book of a tiny hummingbird hovering above a branch of white blossoms. "She weighs less than a dime! Her eggs are only as big as a coffee bean!"

She put the book down and looked at me dreamily. "It looks like we'll have to go to Cuba, because that's where these little treasures live."

Past the café and under the stained glass dome is the sweeping staircase to the second floor. But there's a red rope across the stairs and a sign directing people to the elevator. This is a new development. Katie and I always took the stairs up. When we climbed up or down, she would pretend she was Marie Antoinette or Scarlett O'Hara. I pause there, frowning. I don't like things like this to change. With each thing Katie liked or did disappearing, eventually she'll disappear completely, too.

"Elevator's to your right," a stern voice says from behind me.

The security guy.

"Why did they block the stairs?"

"Kids," he says, as if that explains everything.

He waits until I turn toward the elevator before he walks away.

Upstairs is less old-fashioned than downstairs. Rows of computers take up the middle, and the sound of people hitting the keyboards sends out a constant *clickety clack*. Mothers read Dr. Seuss softly to little kids flopped across beanbag chairs or whooshing fire trucks and other rescue vehicles across the alphabet rug. In other words, it's kind of noisy up there, for a library, anyway.

I find a seat at one of the long tables where people are looking at actual books. Downstairs, the tables are big heavy things, wooden with dark-red leather tops. But these are like the tables at school: light fake wood, modern, bland. I've come to rewrite my poem. Since I left school yesterday with my pretend stomachache, I missed the rest of peer editing, so I have the opportunity to start over. Mom is at Basic Sewing and Dad is at the Art of Collage, and after much pleading, they agreed I could come to the library instead of sitting in the corner of Forget-Me-Knot.

First, I reread the Elizabeth Bishop poem about the fish for inspiration. Then I open a new blank document. I've decided to forego the tsunami and use a stormy sea instead. I've also decided to copy Ava's idea and write a sonnet because that's actually easier. There are rules. There are only fourteen lines, and the last two only have to rhyme with each other.

Just as I'm typing *The Stormy Sea* at the top of the page, I hear a soft whimper. Diagonally across from me is a girl about my age. She has short hair, rectangular glasses, and a hoodie with the name of the school where Gilbert goes, and she's crying. Not sobbing. Tears are spilling out from beneath her glasses, and she lets out another little whimper, and all I can think about is how Clementine was so sad that she took all that Advil, and I didn't even realize she was sad enough to do something so incredibly stupid so I couldn't stop her.

But I can stop this girl.

There's a book open in front of her, and tears are plopping onto the pages. I close my eyes for a few seconds and imagine that bright-red cape with the sparkly purple *J* on the back falling onto my shoulders, making me strong and brave, a superhero who can stop someone from taking too many Advil. Or worse.

When I open my eyes, I open my mouth, too, and blurt, "I know what you're thinking, and you can't do it!"

The girl looks over at me, but so do the guy in the backward baseball cap at the end of the table and the woman in the business suit diagonally across from my other side.

"Her," I say, pointing at the girl. "I'm talking to her."

The woman frowns, and the guy shrugs and goes back to whatever he's doing.

"Me?" the girl says, pointing at herself.

"You're not alone," I tell her. "I know how desperate you feel. I do. But no matter what has happened, no matter how awful, people care about you. *I* care about you."

"Um," she says. "Do I know you? Do you go to Holbrook?"

Should I say it? *Jude Banks, Superhero?*

"Because I'm in Mr. Labinowitz's class, and I have to finish yet another heartbreaking book and write a paper on it," she says.

Mr. Labinowitz? Wasn't that the name of Gilbert's English teacher?

She holds up a book I've never heard of as proof of why she is crying. "I mean, it's really nice and very weird that you're all concerned about me, but if you don't mind . . ."

The woman in the business suit is staring at me in a way that makes me feel like she is about to get the librarian or that security guard, so I smile at her, which makes her look even more freaked out.

The girl is reading her book again, and new tears are falling down her cheeks, and the guy in the backward baseball cap says in a quiet, firm voice, "Hey, kid, maybe you can take it somewhere else."

It takes me a moment to realize he means that I should move my seat.

I gather my things and get up, but as I pass by him, I say, "People do bad things because they don't have any hope."

He doesn't answer, and of course I don't look back to see what the woman in the business suit or the girl from Holbrook are doing. I don't find a new seat, either. Instead, I take the stupid elevator downstairs. I choose a book at random from the pile of books that are only for looking at there, at the library, and I go to the café.

The book is about cats.

Abyssinian. Himalayan. Maine coon.

"Look," I say softly, pointing to a picture of a tan striped cat. "The Manx. It has no tail!"

Then I put my head on the sticky table and cry.

Text I Sent Clementine That She Didn't Answer

I hope you're doing okay???

CHAPTER
TWENTY-ONE

My sonnet, "Stormy Sea," was terrible. Cliché. Weak rhymes. Dumb. But I handed it in, anyway.

"Is that a sonnet?" Ava said as I gave it to her, because she was, of course, the paper collector. "You copied me!"

"I don't think you own sonnets, Ava," I said.

She glared at me before continuing down the row.

I didn't care. I felt about as miserable as a person could feel. Mom was having a bad day, Katie's clothes were cut up all over the house, and Clementine was ghosting me. At least, I thought she was ghosting me. How long does a person stay in the hospital after they have their stomach pumped? Google said twenty-four hours, and it had been lots more than that. What did the wrath of Ava Morton-Wicke matter in the grand scheme of things?

Somehow I got through another miserable day—

fish sticks and peas, intro to volcanoes (strato, shield, and dome), more negative numbers, Sacagawea: Shoshone explorer—and made my miserable way home.

When I saw Gilbert waiting for me in front of my house, my spirits lifted ever so slightly.

"Hey," I said.

"Hey," he said back.

"Want to get gelato or something?" I asked him. Gilbert liked gelato more than almost anything.

He shook his head. "Nah. I've got, like, three projects to do."

"I had to write a *poem*," I said.

"That stinks." He tore at his thumbnail, which was what he did when he was nervous, like before a game or a test. He ripped his nails off, slowly.

"So, anyway," he said, concentrating on his nail. "You kind of freaked out Abby James."

"Who?"

"In the library? The girl who didn't need help that you wanted to help?"

"Oh. Her. How do you even know about that?"

"I heard Abby James telling kids about this weird kid

in the library who started Oprah-ing her. And then Sarah Bixby goes, 'That's the kid whose sister died,' and everyone is all, like, creeped out."

"Creeped out? Because Katie died?"

"Jude, you've got to try to act normal again," Gilbert said.

We stood there, Gilbert peeling off his thumbnail and me feeling awkward and like a weirdo.

"She looked sad," I said finally.

"Look," Gilbert said. "Just try to be normal. Just try."

"Are you kidding me?" I said, indignant.

Gilbert finished tearing off his thumbnail, sighed, and said, "So, anyway. Homework." He rolled his eyes. "Sacagawea: Shoshone explorer."

Normally I would tell him we were studying Sacagawea: Shoshone explorer, too. Normally I'd ask him what his other projects were, and maybe complain about Ava thinking she was the only person in the world who had the right to write a sonnet, and maybe even bring up earthquakes or volcanoes.

But instead I said, "Okay, see ya" and went inside my miserable house.

"Did you know that, statistically, people who help others cope better with their grief?" Dad asked me at dinner that night.

I was still feeling weird about Abby James telling everybody at Gilbert's school that I was creepy. And that now I was known as the kid whose sister died. So I just mumbled something back at him.

"Like starting a car service for prom nights so kids don't drink and drive," Dad said. "Or volunteering at a senior center."

Lately, fewer meals had been showing up on our doorstep, and we'd had to fend for ourselves. I guess people figured that after six months, you should be able to cook your own dinner. Or maybe that after six months, you should have *moved on*. They didn't know that things were still bad inside this house, just different bad. If Mom was having a good day, she actually managed to cook. But if not—and who ever knew?—Dad and I survived mostly on pizza or Chinese takeout or scrambled eggs. Dad did not possess very good cooking skills. Mom always said it was because he was too distractible. He'd forget the sauce simmering and burn it, or forget to turn on the oven, or skip a step or two and ruin whatever he was trying to make. That was why tonight we were eating sandwiches for dinner with a side of potato chips. "Potatoes are vegetables, right?" Dad had said as he ripped open the bag and poured them into the bowl Mom used for real vegetables, like string beans or broccoli.

I was afraid of where Dad was going with these statistics, so I decided to come right to the point. "I'm not volunteering at a senior center. Old people kind of scare me."

"Does Granny scare you?" he asked, surprised.

"Not old like Granny. Old like people who have to live in senior housing."

"I'm not suggesting you volunteer at a senior center, Jude," Dad said in his disappointed voice.

I waited to hear what he was suggesting.

"Mom has really found that sewing and quilting have helped her a lot. They distract her and calm her down. Plus, she's doing something creative."

"She's destroying Katie's clothes," I pointed out.

"Not at all! She's turning them into something warm and comforting instead of giving them away."

"But if she gave them away, wouldn't that be helping people? Kids who can't afford clothes?"

Dad sighed, frustrated. "Maybe. But this isn't about Mom's quilting."

"Dad, what is it you want me to do?" I said. "The woodland animals?"

"Knit! Hats for preemies!" he said it like it was the greatest idea since Lewis and Clark asked Sacagawea for help.

He held up a hand as if to stop words from coming out of my mouth.

"Don't say something sexist like that boys don't knit," he said. "There's this kid in Brooklyn who even started a knitting class in his school. I've got the link somewhere..."

He pulled out his phone and started scrolling, but I told him not to bother.

"I wasn't going to say boys don't knit. I was going to say *I* don't want to knit."

"Gloria from City of Angels runs this workshop on Saturday mornings for kids to knit hats for preemies. City of Angels provides the supplies, and Gloria teaches whoever doesn't know how to knit. And after they've knit a certain amount, they all go to the hospital and deliver the hats, and there's even a little ceremony."

"Oh brother," I said under my breath. I was learning that I was not a person who liked little ceremonies.

"In winter, they knit scarves for the homeless and all go out at night and hang them on the fence near the shelter so anyone can just take a scarf," Dad added.

Wait a minute! This was what Clementine and her mother did! Therefore—as Katie liked to say—if I went to that workshop, I would very possibly see Clementine.

"Sounds good," I said.

Dad looked surprised. "It does?"

"Hats. Preemies. Gloria. Yup, sounds good."

"So Saturday morning, during your mom's sewing class . . ."

I took a big bite of my sandwich, which just a few minutes ago had tasted like cardboard but with this bite came alive in my mouth, all mustard and ham and pickles.

"Great idea," I said, talking with my mouth full.

CHAPTER
TWENTY-TWO

A remarkable thing happened between agreeing to go and knit hats for preemies and actually going to knit hats for preemies on Saturday.

On Thursday, I went to school, as usual. Mom was having a bad day. Dad was having a good day. It was raining again, and so he drove me to school, and we talked about things that didn't matter—Scooby-Doo and Velma, and if it rained for one more day, we would break the record for rainfall set in 1956, and whether a hot dog was considered a sandwich (I said yes, he said no). Then we were at school, and I got out of the car without him trying to hug me like he'd never see me again, which was a great relief.

First thing, we had an assembly about studying foreign languages next year. I could feel the beginnings of a real stomachache. Spring was always when they started talking about the next school year, and I realized this was the first time I would start school without Katie. Señora Gomez was talking about Spanish. Did we know that Spanish was the official language of twenty countries? (She listed them all for us, of course.) Did we know that 18.3% of the population of the United States was Hispanic or Latino? Did we know that was almost sixty *million* people? The whole time she spoke, slides of Spanish things, like flamenco dancers and palm trees and cities I didn't recognize, flashed on the screen behind her, and my stomach hurt more and more.

Then Madame LaFleur talked to us about the benefits of learning French. Everything she said, she said in English and then in French. It was totally annoying, but at the end she passed out little miniature chocolate croissants from Trader Joe's. After that, we had to fill out a form and check off which language we preferred. I didn't check either. Instead I wrote underneath the choices that I had no preference.

The best thing about the assembly was it took up gym class, so we didn't have to do any Estonian folk dances. Ms. Landers didn't even mention our poems. Instead, we read a short story about a town that stoned someone to death once a year but held a lottery to pick the person, so for most of the story you think winning is a good thing. Even though the story was pretty creepy, my stomachache started to go away while I was reading it. In History, we played history *Jeopardy!* and in Math, there was a fire drill and Mr. Delaney got flustered by the interruption so he let us play Rummikub when we returned to class. In other words, it was a pretty good day.

Our neighbor Mrs. Darlington gave me a ride home from school, and even though that meant I was surrounded by girls a year younger than me who talked about things I'd never heard of, at least I didn't have to walk in the rain. Plus, no one treated me weird or carefully. The girls mostly ignored me, except for Tory Kelley, who sprayed imaginary cootie spray on me when I squeezed into the back seat. Mrs. Darlington ignored me, too. She just listened to NPR.

The remarkable thing happened at dinnertime.

I was in my room, writing my essay on "The Lottery," which had to have an introductory statement, three to six supporting statements, and a concluding statement on the question, "How does Shirley Jackson's use of setting and description in 'The Lottery' add to the reader's shock and horror?" when my mother called, "Jude! Dinner!" Just like that. Like normal.

I put my pencil down and sat perfectly still.

"Jude! Dinner!"

She did it again, just like that.

I made my way downstairs, and she was standing at the stove draining the big pasta pot.

"Can you set the table?" she said.

"Um. Sure."

I tried not to stare at her or act in any way that might cause her to stop acting normal. I just got out the dishes, napkins, and silverware and put them on the table. I made sure the salt and pepper were sitting there so no one had to get up during dinner to go find them.

The air smelled really good and familiar. It smelled like beef stroganoff. There was my mother, stirring the sour cream into the pot and pouring it all on top of the egg noodles, which she'd put on the red flowered platter. Was it just yesterday that I'd had sandwiches for dinner, with potato chips as my vegetable? Here was beef stroganoff on top of egg noodles on top of the red flowered platter. Here were green beans shiny with butter. Here was Mom putting dinner on the table.

Even more remarkable was that we three—Mom, Dad, and me—ate that dinner and no one cried or stared off into space or left the table. Dad asked Mom if she had liked Scooby-Doo when she was a kid, and she said she liked Bugs Bunny, Elmer Fudd, and Porky Pig. As she remembered each one, she said something in a different funny voice, like, "That's all, folks!" that made Dad laugh. I told them about the three kinds of volcanoes, and we all tried to figure out which kind Mount Vesuvius was, and before I knew it, I was clearing the table and Dad was scooping ice cream for dessert and we were all sitting around the table eating chocolate-chip cookie dough and it was so sweet and so good that I said, "This is remarkable."

I wondered if they knew I wasn't really talking about the ice cream.

Texts I Wrote to Clementine and Didn't Send

> Guess who's going to knit hats for preemies??? 👀 😋 🙄

> I really can't wait to see you tomorrow at Forget-Me-Knot. Your friend in misery, Jude

> Will you be at Forget-Me-Knot tomorrow? 🙏 🙏 🙏

> Please be at Forget-Me-Knot tomorrow.

CHAPTER
TWENTY-THREE

I knew it was too much to expect Mom to have two good days in a row. Sure enough, Friday wasn't just a bad day, it was a Horrible Day. The sound of her sobbing woke me up, and it only got worse from there. I glimpsed her as I came out of the bathroom and she looked wild, like an animal, her eyes glassy and too big and her hair uncombed. Part of me wanted to go into her room and hug her and remind her that I was still there, that I'd never ever leave her, even though wouldn't Katie have made the same promise? And look what had happened.

Instead I followed the other part of me, the part that didn't want to see my mother crazy with grief. I slipped past her door and down the steps as quietly as possible and practically ran out the door to school. I don't think it was a coincidence that Gilbert and his dad showed up that evening, Gilbert still in his smelly soccer clothes, and invited me to go for pizza with them. What I think is that Mom was having such a horrible day that Dad arranged to get me out of the house. If that was true, I am forever grateful to him. I wanted to get out of there, too.

But Saturday morning, Mom appeared in the kitchen, hair combed, eyes puffy and red from so much crying, wearing clothes that didn't look rumpled, and carrying her Forget-Me-Knot sewing bag, a big canvas thing stuffed with cut-up triangles of Katie's clothes and scissors and needles and thread and a weird thing that looked like a small tomato with pins sticking out of it. She was ready for her Basic Sewing class.

As Dad had mentioned, Gloria was teaching this knitting class. Gloria, I was coming to realize, was one of these people who was competent at everything. She could probably change a flat tire, hang a picture nice and straight on a wall, bake a perfect cake. Mom took a seat at one of the sewing machines that lined one side of the store, and I went into the room where Gloria stood grinning by the door.

Inside were a few kids I recognized from City of Angels—a girl whose name I didn't remember, a boy who never talked, two girls who were somehow involved in a terrible tragedy in which many of their family members died. Tara and Mitch arrived right after I did, and in no time Gloria was handing out knitting needles and a basket of yarn.

"Choose the color that makes you happiest," she said. "You are going to knit love and joy into every stitch for these little babies."

I chose yellow because it made me think of sunshine and lemons and smiley faces.

"As I said in my email to your parents, research shows that volunteerism can have a positive impact on you and your grief, especially when you volunteer for altruistic reasons," Gloria explained. "But research also acknowledges that it's difficult to be out in the world, make new friends, and put yourself out there when you're grieving. That's why doing something together like this can be so helpful. No talking necessary. No need to meet new people. But you get to do something that is really appreciated and helps these little guys who need something warm and cozy. Win-win, right?"

I raised my hand.

"Jude?"

"Is this everybody?" I asked.

"Well, I said in my email that we'd start at ten," Gloria said. She was wearing that gray hat again, so I guess she only took it off when things were really bad. "And it's five minutes after, so I think so."

What a dope I was! Why would Clementine come to this class after what she'd done? How could I have been so hopeful? I tried to concentrate on what Gloria was saying about knitting, how we were just going to move stitches from one needle to the other, over and over, how the Craft Yarn Council lists knitting as an excellent stress reliever. I watched the two tragic girls—one with a ponytail that moved up and down as she knit and the other with a small, fake tattoo of a dragonfly on her wrist—clumsily stick one needle into a stitch, wrap the yarn, and pull. If they could sit there and knit, then I should be able to do it, too, to let the meditative quality of repetitive motion relax me like Gloria said it would.

At the end of the hour, we all had various degrees of a finished hat. At least I wasn't the worst one. Gloria had to keep pulling out all of the knitting of the boy who never talked, and he only had a very few rows done at all.

"Who wants to take their knitting home and work on it this week?" Gloria said in a way that let us know that's what she wanted us to do. Only the boy who never talked dropped his into the basket. I had a feeling he wouldn't come back, and who could blame him? Everyone else shoved theirs into a Forget-Me-Knot bag and took it home with them, including me.

But I didn't leave right away. I waited for Miranda to pick out more yarn. Her hat was practically finished, and she wanted to start a new one right away. Then the tragic girl with the ponytail came back in because she'd lost her phone, and I helped her and Gloria look for it. She was just starting to panic when the girl with the fake tattoo called to her that she had it. Finally, it was just me and Gloria and lots of yarn.

"What's up?" she said.

"I'll tell you what's up," I practically shouted. "Clementine. Where is she?"

Through the open doorway, I could see the people in Basic Sewing who had started to gather their things glance over at me. But my mother just kept on sewing.

"Where is she?" I said again, softer. I dropped back into a chair. Sometimes, like now, I just felt so impossibly heavy.

"Oh, sweetie," Gloria said and sat in a chair next to me. "This has been hard for you, hasn't it? What happened with Clementine, I mean."

"How could she do that?" I said, and my throat got all dry and the words choked their way out. Which was maybe a good thing, because I almost said: *How could she do that to me?*

"She's in a special hospital," Gloria said. "A place that can help her right now more than we can."

It took a minute for this to sink in. She wasn't in a regular hospital? They probably pumped her stomach and sent her . . . where? The psych ward, like on *Grey's Anatomy*?

"Like a mental hospital?" I managed to ask.

"Not exactly," Gloria said. "More like a therapeutic hospital."

I imagined Clementine in a wheelchair, maybe, pale and weak, with a kind nurse pushing her around a garden.

"That's good."

"I can talk to her mother," Gloria said. "Maybe you can visit Clementine there."

Was this actually possible? My heart lifted. If I saw her, I could make her know how much the world needed her in it. I could help her.

"Really?" I managed.

"I'll check, okay?"

I thanked Gloria, and she asked me if I liked knitting, and I told her not really, but I liked the idea of my little yellow hat on some tiny baby's head.

Out in the main room, all the sewing people had left except Mom. She had her head bent over the sewing machine, and she looked determined and like she wasn't going anywhere anytime soon. I sat in one of the easy chairs and watched her sew for the longest time, except I wasn't really watching. I was thinking about Clementine in that wheelchair and that kind nurse and that garden filled with sunflowers and butterflies.

Jude Banks, Superhero

People think they are safest at home. But they're not. Every single day in the United States, six kids die from getting hurt in their own houses, even in their own beds. No one worries about their kid drowning at home, but drowning in the bathtub is the leading cause of death for little kids at home. *In the bathtub.* A girl in Newark, New Jersey, was jumping on her bed, fell out of the window, and died. Another kid in Kansas jumped on the bed, fell, and a pen pierced him, and he died. Kids suffocate and accidentally drink cleaning products or eat medicine that looks like candy. Home is not a safe place. I read all of this stuff on the internet somewhere.

If I could, I would put on my red cape with the sparkly purple *J* on the back and fly around the world draining bathtubs and closing windows and putting away cleaning products and locking medicine cabinets. I would sit all night by the side of kids with hidden heart conditions and watch them as they sleep, watch the steady rise and fall of their chests when they breathe, listen to their little snores and sighs. I would keep every one of them safe and alive. If I could.

CHAPTER
TWENTY-FOUR

I was sitting at the kitchen table, pretending to do my homework. But really I was dunking Oreos into milk until the cookie got so soft it almost—almost—fell into the glass, and then I'd real quick open my mouth and catch it. Many people believe the best way to eat an Oreo is to unscrew the top layer from the bottom, lick off the cream filling, then eat each cookie layer. I, on the other hand, believe soaking them in milk until they almost fall apart is far superior. You get the chocolate cookie, cream filling, and milk flavor all mushed together in one delicious bite. You also get a mess, which was what Mom found when she came into the kitchen—milk and disintegrated cookie on the table and floor and even on my shirt.

"Jude. Seriously?" she said.

She was holding a stack of folded dish towels, which

was a very good thing. It meant she'd done the laundry. For weeks, maybe months, Mrs. Rose, the old arthritic widow down the street, had quietly come into the house and did our laundry. "It's something I can do to help," she had explained when my father found her folding sheets one afternoon. "A little thing." It was Mrs. Rose who did the load of laundry that was sitting in the laundry basket when Katie died, all of our socks and underwear and stained shirts waiting there like nothing unusual had occurred. "It broke my heart," Mrs. Rose had said, "folding your dear sister's happy-colored shirts and things."

"It helps me think," I said, trying to remove Oreo from my teeth with my tongue.

Mom shot me a *You're not fooling me* look that made me grin, Oreo-covered teeth and all. Whenever I glimpsed the person she was before Katie died, my heart lifted.

"Wipe it up," Mom said, and I grinned even bigger. A mother who cared about crumbs on the table was a normal mother.

Mom frowned. "What's funny?"

Mom was like an exotic bird—she had to be handled with care. If I told her I was just happy that she was acting normal, it might send her into a fit of guilt for not being normal. Or sadness that she could act normal when Katie was dead.

So I just pointed to my social studies book open before me and said, "Volcanoes."

"Volcanoes? Are funny?" Mom said, shaking her head.

"Well, not volcanoes, exactly." I glanced at the pages. "Pompeii."

"Jude!" Mom said. She made a clucking noise of disapproval with her tongue and started putting away the dish towels and taking out pans.

I went back to work answering the questions in the book about Pompeii. It was boring to answer the questions in the book, especially about something so dramatic. Imagine being asleep, minding your own business, and all of a sudden being buried in volcanic ash.

"It must have been terrible," Mom said. She was chopping onions, carrots, and celery into perfect little squares. "All that molten lava and—"

"Ash," I corrected her. "First there was an explosion, and smoke poured out from Mount Vesuvius, and people thought that was it. Then there was a *huge* explosion, and the top of the mountain actually blew right off, and ash rained down on Pompeii and covered it in a matter of minutes."

Mom started sautéing. "Is that what your book says?"

"Then there was a *third* explosion that sent ash and stones six miles up into the sky, which covered the city, and buildings started falling, and people were trying to flee—"

"Okay, okay," Mom said. "Stop now. I get it."

But I couldn't stop. "Then that night, six waves of explosions sent even more stuff down on Pompeii and suffocated people and literally baked people—"

"Oh, Jude," Mom said, and she sat down heavily in the chair beside me. "How much sadness can people bear? I mean, how much are we supposed to take?"

"This was so long ago," I said quickly, as if bad things only happened two thousand years ago, even though we knew that right in our home, our safe, loving home, bad things happened.

Mom had her head bent, and her hands covered her face.

"The year seventy-nine!" I said for emphasis.

Mom took two deep breaths. She uncovered her face and looked at me.

"I know," she said wearily.

Slowly she got up and went back to the stove, but she seemed confused there, as if she couldn't remember what she was supposed to do. I went back to answering the questions in the book.

"Oh," Mom said after a while, "I almost forgot to tell you that you can go visit that girl from City of Angels. The one who, you know."

"I can?"

"Her mother called and said the doctor thought it was a good idea, and that visiting hours are from two to five, so maybe I can take you tomorrow?" Mom said.

"Okay," I said.

What did archaeologists find when they discovered the city of Pompeii almost two thousand years after it was destroyed?

Archaeologists discovered that the city of Pompeii was mostly preserved under the ash and debris.

I chewed my pen and thought about that. If Pompeii could be preserved after it was destroyed, maybe people could be okay, too, under all the ash and debris that covered us?

CHAPTER
TWENTY-FIVE

On the ride to the weirdly named Strawberry Patch ("It used to be a strawberry farm," Clementine told me later), I imagined that Clementine would be in an orange jumpsuit, behind Plexiglas. That I'd have to talk to her by telephone, a big, heavy black one, like from the olden days. ("It's not prison," she said crankily when I told her that.) Mom and I drove past cranberry bogs and over a bridge and down a winding road with the glistening bay to our right. Then, through a small entryway flanked with stone pillars and onto a gravel driveway, green fields as far as you could see and that bright bay in the distance.

Inside, Strawberry Patch looked like a series of living rooms with furniture like Granny had—flowered chairs and dark-wood everything—with a desk plunked in the middle. At that desk sat a woman who looked like Elton

John: small, chubby, and short-haired with enormous glasses. My heart squeezed tight. Katie would have loved hearing that—*a woman who looked like Elton John! Brilliant!*

But Mom was using her all-business voice, and I didn't have time to dwell on my brilliance or Katie. As soon as Mom said, "Jude Banks is here to visit Clementine Marsh," Elton John was up out of her swivel chair and telling us to *come this way.*

Right there in one of the living rooms, Clementine sat in a chair with golden and burnt-orange flowers, in front of a table with a mostly unfinished jigsaw puzzle on it. As soon as she saw me, she jumped up and threw her arms around me.

"Jude! Jude!" she said, over and over.

Once apart, she threw her arms out dramatically. "Look what I've become! A jigsaw-puzzle doer!"

The puzzle was of some famous painting of blurry lilies in a blurry blue pond. I think Doctor Botticelli had shown me that one.

Mom had disappeared, and it seemed like Clementine and I were the only people in all of Strawberry Patch.

I tried not to stare at Clementine, but I couldn't help myself. Here she was! Even here, her hair was shampoo-ad shiny, and her skin was clear and her eyes were bright. In other words, she seemed absolutely herself and absolutely fine.

"Oh, Jude," Clementine said, "it was so dumb!"

She flopped onto the couch, and I sat on the chair across from her.

"It was, like, a moment of despair. Less than a moment. A nanosecond," Clementine said. "You know how it is, that feeling, that horrible feeling of, 'How can I possibly go on?'"

I did know that feeling. The way it hit you that your parents weren't the same, that nothing was the same, and that nothing would ever be the same again. That feeling of utter disbelief that your sister was dead, and that dead meant not coming back. Ever. There was just emptiness, silence, and a long, dark tunnel into the future.

"I know," I managed to say.

"I mean, seriously. Advil. If I wanted to really do it, I would throw myself off a bridge or something. I'd at least be dramatic."

"Of course you would," I said, taking an odd comfort in this. Advil was so ordinary, so common, that someone like Clementine would never use it if she were seriously trying to kill herself.

"It's not too bad here," Clementine was saying. "I have to go to all these *therapy* sessions, like City of Angels, except City of Angels is so much better. And I have to work outside in the garden because they believe fresh air is curative. And I have to keep a journal, except unlike *real* journals, everybody around here gets to read it."

I nodded, surprised by how simple her treatment was. No electric shocks or straitjackets or solitary confinement.

"The woman at the desk?" I said. "She looks like Elton John." Clementine's mother, like my father, was a huge Elton John fan. She and Halley grew up listening to his albums, just like Katie and I did.

"She does! I knew she looked familiar!" Clementine said and burst into delighted laughter.

"Rocket man!" I said.

"Stop!" Clementine said gleefully.

After we'd caught our breath, we were silent until I said, "When are you coming home, anyway?"

Clementine let out a long, slow breath. "When they think I won't do anything stupid like that again."

"That's easy," I said. "You would never!"

Was I imagining it, or did Clementine take the slightest pause before she flashed her toothpaste-ad smile at me and said, "Never!"

Things I Would Tell You about Katie

She was the one that people on the street or in stores stopped to gush over. "Isn't she adorable?" they might say. Or, "She's going to take over the world someday, isn't she?"

I could even remember being in our double stroller and waiting patiently for Katie to be adored. Usually, I didn't get mentioned at all. Though sometimes I might get my hair tousled or a "You're a cutie, too," delivered dutifully.

The thing is, I never cared. Mom always checked in with me. "Jude," she'd say, "Katie is just one of those people who grabs attention wherever she goes. You know you're superspecial, too, don't you?" I did know that. But I also knew that Katie *was* adorable. She *was* going to take over the world someday. I was proud that she was my sister. Proud to sit on the other side of the stroller with her. Proud to be in her orbit.

I didn't care that lots of times, people referred to me as Katie's brother instead of by my name. On carousels, Katie somehow always got the golden ring; she always scored the hole in one at mini golf; she guessed the answer to twenty questions in ten or under questions; and she always got the wild card, the lucky number, the newest penny.

That was just Katie.

She was special. Blessed, even. Until she wasn't.

CHAPTER
TWENTY-SIX

Weeks passed, and still Clementine did not appear at City of Angels or Forget-Me-Knot. She didn't answer my texts, either. Every day I found myself imagining her at Strawberry Patch, sitting in one of those ugly flowered chairs and working on a jigsaw puzzle. But how long did she have to be there before they decided she could come home? Why weren't they convinced she would never do anything this stupid again? I thought about visiting again, but it was so complicated—my mother calling her mother, the hour-and-fifteen-minutes ride each way, all of it.

Ms. Landers was talking about the *epistolary* novel, which was a novel written entirely in letters. She passed around a bunch of them—*The Perks of Being a Wallflower*, *Flowers for Algernon*, and *Dracula*. At the end of this unit, we were all going to read *Frankenstein*, but today we had to break into four groups and look through one of these books and then write a letter together, like we were one of the characters.

I hated breaking into groups. Groups were always the same: There was always someone who took charge, bossing the others around and taking credit for everything. There was always someone who liked to draw and would offer to make a book cover or something and then just sit there looking all dreamy with their colored pencils and sketch pad, not contributing even one thought or comment. What really bothered me about the artist person was that when they finally finished their masterpiece, everybody made such a big fuss over it. All the hard work of the worker bees—like me—who did research and came up with stuff and got bossed around was not gushed over at all. Of course, there was always one person who did nothing except maybe make fart jokes or play with a fidget spinner or even doze off while everyone else did the dumb project.

But when you're put into a group for a project, you have to accept your fate. For me, that meant I would do all the boring bits and get no credit for anything. I would let Lizzie Lu take over and assign jobs and complain that she was doing *all the work*. Valerie Coccinelle would sit there, with her ridiculous amount of pencils and markers, and draw flowers, and Jake Castille would do nothing but annoy us all. Our group's book was *Flowers for Algernon*, a totally depressing story about some poor guy named Charlie with a super-low IQ who gets thrown into this experiment that ends up making him smart, only to have it reverse after he's fallen in love and made a happy new life.

Lizzie made me and the other drones read the letters Charlie writes in the book out loud and present a synopsis to the group. But my mind kept wandering. I didn't like group projects, but I didn't like this group or this project most of all. Jake Castille smelled like he hadn't washed his socks, the book was sad, and I kept getting the urge to sweep all of Valerie Coccinelle's art supplies off the table and onto the floor.

I am 32 yeres old and next munth is my brithday. I tolld dr Strauss and perfesser Nemur I cant rite good . . .

I sighed. There was no way I could undo Charlie's fate, no way to make this a good story. For a moment, I got angry with Katie because the only reason they put me in Honors

English was because she was in Honors English. But she belonged here. Most of the projects made my brain hurt.

"Jude?" Lizzie said. "Are you reading or taking notes or what?"

"I want to get smart if they will let me," I read out loud, then I gave her a look like I was hugely insulted.

"I'm handling a lot here," Lizzie said. "All you have to do is read, like, thirty pages and take notes."

"I *am*," I lied and picked up my pencil.

But instead of writing about poor Charlie, I wrote:

Dear Clementine,

Are you still at Strawberry Patch? Did you finish that puzzle? I really liked seeing all the cranberry bogs when we drove to see you. Fog was hanging over them, and they looked beautiful. I am still knitting hats for preemies on Saturdays, but my hats don't look like hats. They look like lumps with holes in them. I hope the babies don't mind.

"Jake, look how hard Jude is working," Lizzie said. "Are you writing anything down at all?"

I have to read a very depressing book called <u>Flowers for Algernon</u>. Have you read it? It's an epistolary novel, which means it's written in letters instead of in regular prose. I think I like the other, usual way better.

"Oh my, Valerie, those flowers are so beautiful," Lizzie cooed. "I love the colors. Honestly, you are going to live in Paris or somewhere and become a famous artist, I just know it."

I'd like to come visit again if I can get my mom or dad to drive me there. They are so busy trying to stay busy so they don't have to think about Katie that they hardly have time for anything. But I can beg them. Does that sound good?

Your friend,

Jude

I Mailed The Letter
and Clementine Answered!

Dear Jude,

Writing letters is so old—fashioned! I kind of
love it! Actually, receiving your letter was very
dramatic. I was involved in a very boring, not
very competitive game of Scrabble, bored to
tears, when Margaret, aka Elton John, walks
into the solarium waving this envelope and
calling my name. "Mail!" she says. "Mail!" She is
so excited that her eyes are practically popping
out of her head. "Mail!" Apparently, until a few
years ago, every morning she would put all the
mail on this little cart like flight attendants use
for beverages, and she'd go up and down the
halls and into all the public rooms and call,

"mail! mail!" and everyone would be excited to see her and even more excited if there was a letter or a card in there for them. But these days it practically never happens. People do not write letters anymore, Margaret told me, and honestly I thought she was going to cry, except she was so happy to bring me your letter that she didn't actually cry. I think everyone else in that room was extremely jealous. I mean, I got a letter!

Your friend,
Clementine

PS: I never got your texts because we aren't allowed to have phones here! I meant to tell you that when you visited!

CHAPTER
TWENTY-SEVEN

I was at City of Angels, miserable because I didn't want to be there. Without Clementine, it wasn't as interesting. Plus, it was an especially dreary night. Not rainy dreary or even sad dreary, but gray and cold dreary. The kind of night when you want nothing more than to stay inside in your jammies, maybe even wrapped in a quilt, doing something like reading a book not required for Honors English, or playing cards with your sister (which of course was impossible). Dad had to work extremely hard to get me into my warm jacket to go to City of Angels.

I was sulking. For one thing, I realized that faces kept changing at City of Angels. Kids came and went, sometimes really fast. The tragic sisters didn't come anymore. Neither did the girl who smelled like Christmas trees or the girl whose sister got electrocuted by her blow-dryer.

Where did they all go? Were they suddenly *over it*? Had they *moved on*? That's what everyone was always suggesting we do, which seemed impossible to me. But maybe these kids had somehow managed to actually get over it and move on.

What made me sad was that there was always a new kid in that empty seat. In other words, kids just kept on dying, and there were always siblings getting ripped apart. Tonight, for example, there were six—six!—new kids and six new, sad, sad stories—a tonsillectomy gone wrong; a genetic disease; a scooter accident; a long, horrible cancer; and two cases of something called sudden infant death syndrome. I did not want to hear one more sad story.

Even more confusing were the kids who had been coming for years. Were they stuck forever in the horrible grief that enveloped me? Was there no hope for, if not getting over it or moving on, then at least feeling better enough to not want to come out on a dreary night and talk about death and grief? Were their lives now defined by their sister or brother dying? How did I know that wasn't my own fate? That no one at school would ever look me in the eye again? That I would never be able to walk past

Katie's room without wanting to cry? That my parents would be stuck in the good day/bad day cycle forever?

All of these thoughts were swirling around my brain when the door opened and, just like that, Clementine walked in. It was like a sunbeam arrived. The whole room changed from sad and dreary to bright and, well, not cheerful but uplifted.

"Clementine!" Gloria practically squealed. She jumped up and bounced a little on her toes. "Welcome back."

One of the girls who had been at City of Angels forever motioned for Clementine to come and sit beside her.

It is not an exaggeration to say that once Clementine arrived, everything got better.

She even took the angel thing and said, "Wow, lots of new faces. So, I'm Clementine. As you know." That little blush again. "I just wanted to say that even though we have had the most terrible thing that can happen to a person happen to us, we still have parents and maybe other siblings and friends who love us, and when we feel utter sadness, we need to remember all those people who love us and hold on to that because that's about the most important thing in the whole world."

A few kids actually applauded. Lots of kids nodded. One of the new kids—scooter accident—actually wrote something down in one of those notebooks with a shiny cover that changes when it moves.

Clementine smiled and took a deep breath and said, "That's what I wanted to say."

Then she looked directly at me, and maybe you don't know what it feels like when a beam of sunshine on a dreary night sends its light onto you. But I do.

Things I Would Tell You about Katie

All of a sudden, I realized that when your only sister dies, she takes about half of your memories with her. Katie and I did things together that no one else did or even knew about. I have memories of Katie at school, memories of Katie with our parents, memories of Katie on playdates, memories of Katie doing public things—spelling bees, dance recitals, plays, Halloween parades, visiting Santa at the mall. I figure that's about 50 percent of my Katie memories. Which means 50 percent of my memories are of Katie and me. Which means that 50 percent will be gone, because I'm the only one in the entire world who has them.

Like the day she drank the ink out of a pen just to see what ink tasted like, and then we got worried that maybe ink was poisonous, so she ate a whole loaf of bread because she thought that lots of bread got rid of poison, and then she threw up blue bread.

She also ate ants, soap, a crayon, and paper just to see what they tasted like.

Once she took gum from a 7-Eleven and then felt so guilty that she put it back. Unshoplifting, she called it.

She kept a hermit crab in her nightstand drawer until it started to stink.

She kept a log of all the books she'd ever read, all the way back to *Goodnight Moon*, with notes about what she thought about them.

We invented our own routine of snapping and slapping and saying nonsense words that not even one other person knows except for me.

One day, after Mom told me to put on some shoes if I was going to be outside on the deck, because Dad needed to sand it because there were so many splintery pieces of wood, I went out on the deck barefoot, anyway, and I got a giant splinter in my foot. And instead of getting me in trouble for going out on the deck barefoot after Mom told me not to, Katie got the tweezers, sterilized them with a match, and as tenderly as possible, she got that splinter out of my foot, and Mom never knew.

On Halloween last year, Katie and I stayed up all night and ate all the candy we wanted.

She used to eat my peas, and I ate her green beans.

When we had "How long can you hold your breath under water?" contests, I always won.

She liked to fart in the bathtub when we used to take baths together, just to make me laugh.

Katie was working on an invention: a peanut butter jar that opened on both ends so that when you reached the bottom, instead of getting your hand all peanut buttery to get out the last bits, you just had to turn the jar upside down, open that end, and voilà! The peanut butter was right there.

She was also working on an umbrella with a light on the handle so that you could see puddles at night.

Maybe I should start writing these down in a notebook so that I never forget them? Because otherwise, when I get older and my mind has collected more facts and ideas and new memories, how else can I guarantee that I will never, ever forget the Katie-and-me memories? That's what Katie would do. She had notebooks for everything. She would be sure to remember.

CHAPTER
TWENTY-EIGHT

When someone dies, people do all kinds of weird things. For example, I cannot even begin to count how many angel-themed things people sent us when Katie died. First of all, no one wants to think of his sister as an angel. That does not make anybody feel better. Angels are dead. And even though technically I knew that Katie had died, thinking of her as an angel made me feel worse. Angels wear white robes, play harps, and have halos around their heads. Sisters don't have any of that.

Another weird thing is that we got all these plaques with creepy sayings on them, like the one that had a picture of a beach and footprints in the sand and a poem about accepting the things we can't have, which when I read it, I was like: Are you kidding me? I will never, ever, ever accept that I can't have Katie anymore. I also don't

take any comfort in the idea that I will see her again—
in heaven. Great. Then I'll be dead, too, and Katie and I will
sit on our clouds and play our stupid harps together.

Luckily, Mom and Dad also hated all these plaques
and poems and angels. They all ended up in a box out by
the curb on trash day.

However, they both liked the idea of the school
planting a tree in Katie's memory. And of attending the
tree-planting ceremony.

"A tree?" I said.

"Trees grow and bloom," Mom said sadly. "They live a
long time."

"Okay," I said. "But why do they have to have a
ceremony? Can't they just plant the tree and call it a day?"

"It's a way to honor Katie," Dad said.

"I don't want to go," I said, even though I knew that
the whole point of this discussion was to tell me that I had
to go.

"We're still a family, Jude," Dad said. "And this is
something we should do as a family. For Katie."

What I didn't say was, *Do you honestly think Katie
would want everybody in school to stand around while*

Mr. Jameson, the custodian, planted a tree in her memory? She'd be mortified.

"I think it's really thoughtful," Mom said. She was wringing her hands in a way that broke my heart.

"Fine," I said.

That was why on a perfectly fine Sunday afternoon in May, we had to put on dressy clothes and drive in sad silence to school to stand there and watch Mr. Jameson plant a tree next to the front entrance.

I was shocked at how many people had turned up for this thing. I mean, the schoolyard was packed with kids and parents and teachers, who all grew absolutely quiet when we walked up the path. Every head turned and looked at us with these super-sad eyes and a lot of pity. *Poor family,* they were all thinking. *That's the kid whose sister died.* I wanted to run back to the car and hide. But, of course, I didn't. I stayed right in between Mom and Dad, all the way to where Mr. Jameson and also the principal and vice principal and even Nurse Barb stood waiting.

They all said kind things to Mom and Dad, but I didn't want to listen. Instead, I looked at who the heck had come to such a depressing thing as a tree-planting ceremony for a kid who had died. Of course, my whole class was there. And Ms. Landers and all of my other teachers and even the Spanish and French teachers who I didn't really know. Everyone wore solemn expressions and dark clothes. I was surprised when the school band started playing "Ode to Joy," and even more surprised that the song made some people start to cry, including Mom.

Then the principal gave a little talk about trees and Katie and longevity and a bunch of other stuff. I stopped listening because even though I was standing there with all these people and right in front of me was Mr. Jameson with a tree waiting to be planted, it seemed pretty unreal. It was weird to hear the principal talking about Katie like she was dead, and even weirder that she was dead.

Next thing I knew, Mom was at the microphone, and she was crying, but softly, and she was thanking everyone in a quivering voice, and then she was reading the Robert Frost poem "The Master Speed." Panic started to rise in my chest, like a big, heavy thing that threatened to crush me or maybe explode out of me. Don't cry, I ordered myself. Do not cry in front of all these people.

Mr. Jameson took a shovel and dug through the earth, and then, oddly, Mom and Dad each took a turn with the shovel. Next thing I knew, Dad was handing the shovel to me, but I didn't want to do it, to take that shovel and dig. All of a sudden, images from the funeral swept over me like a tsunami: the white coffin with the brightly colored flowers on the top; the way Mom's high heels got stuck in the soft grass when she walked, which made her stagger slightly; Gilbert looking terrified; Dad keeping his hands on the coffin like he could somehow still touch Katie; that governor's obelisk looming; the crying. All the crying. So loud and so hard that it felt like the ground was shaking.

Somehow, the moment passed. Mr. Jameson had taken the shovel from Dad, and the band was playing that song "Feelin' Groovy," which made Mom smile even though she was still crying. I knew that Mom thought that was Katie's favorite song still, but really it had been her favorite song when we were little.

Hello, lamppost! What'cha knowing? I've come to watch your flowers growing . . .

The words were filling the air. I mean, the whole

crowd spontaneously started singing the song, and their voices rose up and up and up into the sky, where maybe the angels could hear them, where maybe even an eleven-year-old girl sitting on a cloud could hear them.

"Feelin' groovy!" the voices sang, lifting upward.

Jude Banks, Superhero

A teenager in Manchester, England, died at a nightclub from a too-loud bass. He said to his friend, "That bass is making my heart feel weird," and then he dropped down dead.

A six-year-old girl in Toronto died when an alarm clock went off.

A college sophomore taking a nap in his fraternity's common room died when music from the next room blasted on. "I walked past him, and he was breathing and everything, and then somebody put on rock music and I happened to glance down at him, and I could tell he'd stopped breathing, and I tried CPR, but he was already gone," his roommate said.

How can I save people like them? Run around colleges and nightclubs and people's houses turning down the volume on everything? Unplugging things? Telling people to be quiet?

I think about how Katie looked that night when I woke up and walked into her room. It wasn't exactly night. It was dawn; the sky outside her window was mostly gray but streaked with pink and violet. And Katie was sound asleep in her purple striped jammies, holding her old stuffed rabbit, Trixie, her hair fanned out around her, the open doorway allowing in just a small, soft amount of light, and Katie and Trixie and her whole room looking so quiet and peaceful and happy, like in "Silent Night" when it goes, *All is calm, all is bright.*

I stood in the doorway, and instead of whispering her name or even just leaving her alone and letting her sleep, I shouted, "Boo!"

That's what I did.

I shouted, "Boo!"

And Katie died.

What Clementine Texted Me and What I Texted Her

Clementine texted me:

> Are you going to Forget-Me-Knot to knit for those poor preemies who only weigh like a pound? Because if you are, maybe we could go next door for burgers afterward?

Of course I texted back immediately:

> Yes!!!

I waited, but that was the end of our texting.

CHAPTER
TWENTY-NINE

Joe's Dairy was actually not a dairy at all. I guess it was owned by a dairy at some point, and it did sell ice cream, and if you ordered milk there, it came out of a big silver container with a tap: plain, chocolate, or coffee. What Joe's Dairy was now was the place everybody's parents took them for lunch when they were little because the menu served only kid food and a bucket of crayons sat on every table and all the placemats had word searches and mazes and pictures to color, like scarecrows or Easter eggs or seashells. It was a place with red-vinyl booths and a curving countertop that sold burgers, hot dogs, and grilled-cheese sandwiches, and everything came with fries and coleslaw and pickles. In other words, Joe's Dairy was perfect.

Clementine and I walked there from Forget-Me-Knot and slid into one of the booths. She immediately started coloring the garden on the placemat. Even when the waitress, who had been working there probably since Joe's Dairy was still a dairy, came over to take our order, Clementine did not look up.

"Double cheeseburger," she said, carefully coloring the carrots orange. I thought about how Katie would have colored them purple or bright blue.

"Joe's sauce? Onions? Lettuce-tomato?" the waitress asked.

Clementine shook her head no.

"Hot dog," I said, making sure to look right at the waitress so she didn't think we were the rudest kids to ever sit in her section.

The Joe's Dairy waitress uniforms were the worst: red-and-white striped with white aprons that had a yellow cow embroidered on them. The cow always creeped out Katie because it was smiling, and, first of all, cows don't smile and, second of all, this cow's smile made it look like it was a killer cow.

I looked at that cow and felt sad while the waitress said, "Meat sauce? Onions?"

"No, thank you," I said and picked up a blue crayon

and started coloring a carrot.

Joe's Dairy had the best hot dogs. They cut them the long way, grilled them, and served them in a buttery, grilled split-top bun. I always got a hot dog, and Katie always got a grilled cheese but only after torturing herself and everybody with her over whether she should get a cheeseburger or a grilled cheese. "Just get the grilled cheese," I'd always beg her. "Please. You know that's what you want." "But the cheeseburger with Joe's sauce," she'd say, studying the menu like she'd never seen it before, "sounds soooo interesting. What's in that sauce, anyway?" And on and on, until we all wanted to scream.

If I stopped coloring and looked around, I knew I would see my parents and Katie and me in that booth over there after Katie's one and only tap-dance recital. She would be still dressed in her sparkly costume and top hat, which was the only reason she took tap classes. There she'd be, saying, "Grilled cheese or cheeseburger . . ." And in that far booth, I'd see a bunch of us squeezed in, blowing the wrappers off straws at one another, after the last day of school. Our mothers would be in a different booth, pretending they didn't know us, and Katie would be saying,

"Grilled cheese or cheeseburger . . ." and I'd scream, "Just get the grilled cheese!"

That was why I kept coloring. This place was haunted.

I almost forgot Clementine was sitting across from me. When she said, "Blue carrots?" she actually startled me.

"My garden has the blues," I said. All that poetry in Ms. Landers's class had gotten to me, I guess.

The waitress plopped our food down and slid the squirt bottles of ketchup, mustard, and relish toward us. She was gone before I could say thanks.

"I've gathered us here today to tell you something," Clementine said. "Something important."

I waited while she squirted ketchup onto her fries and then on both sides of her hamburger bun.

"Do you remember that I told you I killed my sister?" she said, finally.

I nodded. I knew I should say something, something kind, but my throat went so dry so fast that no words could come out. I nodded again, and then looked away. I squirted one wavy line of mustard right down the split of my hot dog.

"There was this guy," she continued, "and his wife had a peanut allergy, and he ate a peanut butter and jelly sandwich for *lunch*, and he went home six hours later, and he kissed her hello, and she *died*."

"From a kiss?" I said.

"Traces of peanut butter," Clementine said in a hushed voice. "On his lips."

"Wow."

We both chewed our food for a moment, then I said, "Is that like what happened to Halley? You had peanut butter on your hands or something?"

"Obviously, we didn't even keep peanut butter in our house. So at school I always sneaked some from the big jar in the kitchen, you know, stuck a spoon in there and ate a big, delicious mouthful."

"At school?" I said, because at my school only the cafeteria ladies went into the kitchen.

"I go to a Montessori," she said, like that explained everything. When I still didn't get it, she explained that it was a whole way of teaching invented by an Italian woman named Maria Montessori, and the kids baked bread and made salads from stuff they grew in a garden and things like that. Instead of cafeteria ladies, parents actually came in and cooked lunch.

"We can go in there for snacks anytime we want, so of course I liked to have some peanut butter because I never, ever got to have it anywhere else. But that day, I couldn't find a spoon, so I stuck a knife in there, and I licked peanut butter off the knife and then I quickly rinsed the knife, and Halley maybe used that knife to cut her sandwich. She just got braces, and she was always cutting things into smaller pieces because her mouth was sore." She leaned back in the booth. "Traces of peanut butter."

"Wait a minute. You said she *maybe* used that knife. Which means maybe she didn't."

"But what else could it be? Where did she get the peanut butter, then? I mean, she wasn't eating a peanut butter sandwich."

"I don't know, but it seems like there's infinite possibilities."

"Like what?"

"Once I got in trouble because I shared my cookies with Gabby Monroe, and she had a peanut allergy, and her lips swelled even though they were chocolate-chip cookies."

Clementine nodded. "That's why you have to always read the ingredients."

"Maybe that happened. Maybe Halley ate someone's cookie."

"She wouldn't do that. When you have a life-threatening allergy, you read the ingredients."

I concentrated on my hot dog.

"Did you know a guy died on an airplane from all the peanut dust in the air from those little bags of peanuts they give you?" Clementine said.

"Maybe that's what happened. Peanut dust from someone's bag of peanuts."

Clementine looked very disappointed in me. I wasn't sure if she wanted me to tell her she had killed her sister by rinsing that knife off instead of scrubbing it of any peanut butter residue, or if she was looking for me to find an alternative scenario.

"I've gone over and over it," she said. "I had A lunch, and Halley had B lunch, so she was in there right after me. I was in math class taking a quiz, and I heard the siren getting closer and closer, and I had three thoughts, all at the same time. Halley. Peanut butter. That knife."

"But—"

"It had happened before at school. And I always rode

with her in the ambulance, not *with* with her but up front, next to the driver, and it was scary, but they gave her a shot and oxygen, and she was always fine. That was why they started peanut-free tables in the lunchroom, so she couldn't even be near peanut butter." She was holding a french fry dripping ketchup onto the table, but she didn't seem to notice. "So then tell me where she got exposed to peanuts."

Before I could answer, Clementine said, "You see, this is what is driving me crazy."

I didn't feel good at all when Clementine's mother showed up to bring her home. She offered to give me a ride, but I explained how my mother was still at Forget-Me-Knot, and I was just going to walk back there.

"All righty then," her mother said with fake cheerfulness, probably because she could see how miserable Clementine looked. "I'm so glad you two had lunch!"

"Yeah, thanks, Jude," Clementine said.

Stop! I wanted to call to her as she walked out. *Remember someone else's cookie! Peanut dust! Maybe there was peanut butter residue on the table! Maybe someone with peanut residue on their hands touched her! Maybe there was peanut butter in something that never has peanut butter, so why would she read the ingredients?*

After what happened next, I wished I had stopped her. I wished I had gone through every single possibility. But I didn't. I just finished my hot dog and watched her and her mother walk away.

Texts I Sent To Clementine That She Didn't Answer

Maybe someone hugged her tight and had peanuts on their breath like that woman whose husband had the sandwich?

I feel like I disappointed you . . .

Did I disappoint you somehow? Let's meet? At the cemetery?

I know how you feel. I do.

Clementine???

More Texts I Sent To Clementine That She Didn't Answer

> The night Katie died,
> I did something terrible.

> Clementine?

> Clementine? You ok?

CHAPTER
THIRTY

I'd never seen a picture of Halley until the night at City of Angels when we were "invited to bring photographs of your siblings." Gloria was always having us do projects like that, things that would help us "keep their memories alive." One night, we had to write down one memory and then read it out loud. I wrote one down, but when it was my turn to read, I said, "Pass." Another time, Gloria asked us to bring in something our siblings had drawn or made. Tara brought in one of those pictures kids draw of stick people and a house and a sun in one corner. Mitch brought in a tie-dyed T-shirt that his brother had made. I didn't bring anything in, and later Gloria told me it was okay not to participate but she really, really thought I would start to feel better if I did.

Since I didn't want to bring in a picture, either,

Dad brought the collage he and Mom had made for the memorial service. I hated that collage. For one thing, it was too bright and happy. All the pictures were of Katie in her sparkly clothes, acting dramatic or silly. Katie in a hot-pink boa and Mom's cat-eye sunglasses with the rhinestones. Katie dressed like a mermaid—shiny, iridescent scales and a tulle tail in blues and greens and silver. Katie with her arm thrown around me, melted red Popsicle around both of our mouths. Katie and me in front of an elaborate sandcastle with moats and turrets; only we knew someone else had built that thing and we were just posing in front of it. Katie in a cotton-candy-pink wig. Katie with her arms wide open and her eyes closed, like she's saying, *Here I am, world!*

To my surprise, other kids brought in collages from their siblings' funerals, too. I guess that was the protocol for funerals; sad parents are forced to sift through pictures of their kid and somehow create a collage from them. But Clementine just brought in two pictures in a double frame, like she'd scooped them off a table or something when she left that evening. In one, Halley and Clementine are toddlers. They're dressed alike—*Mom always did that to us*—but one looks terrified, and the other looks like she's having a blast. I never did find out who was who. The other one looked like it could have been taken that very day. Clementine looks like Clementine, which is to say all shiny and bright, and Halley sits across from her at a turquoise kitchen table, her eyes mischievous and the very slightest smile turning up the corners of her mouth, like she has a secret.

When I'm not thinking about volcanoes or epistolary novels, I'm thinking about that girl with the secret. What did she know that no one else did? That she was about to leave for good? That life is short? Or maybe she, like Katie, didn't have an inkling everything was about to change. Maybe she's just a person who always looks like the cat that swallowed the canary.

❧

The next day at school, it was very hard to concentrate on volcanoes or epistolary novels when all I could think about was dead sisters. Mine, of course. And Clementine's. I went through the morning on autopilot. After lunch, I got caught in the crush of kids heading to their next classes, and I could hardly breathe because there were so many kids and they smelled like the cafeteria sloppy joes and sweat, and that got all mixed in with the smell of the strong disinfectants they used to clean the school. I was getting jostled, like everybody else, but I had the feeling that if one more person bumped into me, crowded me, or pushed past me, I was going to lose it. I imagined myself like that emoji of a head with the top of its skull off and what looks like a nuclear cloud exploding out of it. I imagined myself stopping right there, maybe even causing people to knock into one another and fall down or bounce off the lockers. I imagined chaos, chaos like I'd felt ever since that morning when Dad looked at me and said, "Oh, Jude."

I did it. I stopped right there, and kids did bump into one another and someone muttered, *Asshole*, and someone else said, real loud, *Nice move!* But I didn't care. I stopped walking, and I imagined the top of my head blowing off and that nuclear mushroom cloud exploding out of it. My fists were clenched, and my mouth was open but no sound came out. Did anyone notice that the top of my head blew off? Did anyone feel the chaos from my heart?

I gulped for air. But it was like the crowded corridor sucked up every bit of it. It was like there was no air at all.

I gulped again, and I heard a strangling sound, and then I realized that sound was coming from me because I *could not breathe.*

I clutched my throat like a person dying in a movie, and I tried to yell for help, but black spots were floating in front of my eyes, like when we looked at our skin under a microscope in science class.

"What's he doing?" I heard someone say, and that person sounded not worried at all.

Except, I thought, he should be worried because I *could not breathe.*

Now the black spots were all I saw.

"I think he's having a heart attack!" someone shouted.

Good, I thought. At least she's worried.

"Like his sister," someone else said as I crumpled to the floor.

The person who said that was Ava Morton-Wicke, and my last thought was how terrible it was that the last thing I ever heard was Ava Morton-Wicke being a jerk.

❧

If you're going to get to ride in an ambulance, at least you should get to remember it. That was what I thought when I opened my eyes, realized I wasn't dead, and saw that I was in a hospital bed.

Dad and Mom were sitting right there beside me, and when I opened my eyes, Mom jumped up and said, "Just breathe. Nice, deep breaths."

That was when I realized I had an oxygen mask over my mouth and nose. I had the urge to yank it off, but the look on Mom's face made me decide to do exactly what she wanted me to do. Just breathe. Nice, deep breaths.

"You scared the living daylights out of us, buddy," Dad said. I could tell he was trying to sound upbeat, even lighthearted, but his voice was shaky, like he'd had the living daylights scared out of him.

"Sorry," I said. Or at least, I think I said it. My voice seemed to have gotten really tiny.

"It was a panic attack and getting overheated. That's all," Mom said. She was stroking my hair a little too enthusiastically. "The hallway was hot and crowded, and you kind of fainted."

I hadn't realized that fainting felt like dying.

"Ms. Landers said you were having a bad day," Dad said.

"She did?" I said, surprised. She'd hardly seemed to notice me in class.

A cheerful doctor appeared and flipped through papers on a clipboard that was dangling off the foot of the bed.

"We're going to get you some apple juice and some graham crackers, and then you'll be good to go," he said. He sounded like he was a television announcer: *And the winner is . . .*

Mom was clutching his hand, saying, "Thank you, thank you," like he'd pulled me out of a shark's mouth instead of giving me some oxygen, making sure my vital signs were okay, and telling a nurse to get me some apple juice.

The best part was that I had to leave the hospital in a wheelchair. That was actually hospital policy. Since I'd missed the ambulance ride, I was glad for this opportunity. Dad let me spin around the lobby and even attempt a wheelie before he took over again and wheeled me out to the car. Despite the apple juice and graham crackers and oxygen, I did feel a little shaky.

"You scared the daylights out of us," Mom said, her eyes meeting mine in the rearview mirror.

"So Dad said," I said.

"The hallway was overheated, wasn't it, buddy? And crowded?" Dad said.

"And smelly! All those kids and the cafeteria smell and sweat and stuff."

Both of my parents nodded vigorously. I could practically read their minds. *Our kid is fine! He just had a panic attack in that hot, crowded, smelly hallway!* I understood that these things brought them comfort.

We were almost home before I said, "I thought I was dying."

Mom's head whipped around. "Oh, sweetie. It was scary, wasn't it?"

I nodded.

Mom patted my knee. "You're okay now."

"Do you think that's how Katie felt?" I said.

As soon as the words were out of my mouth, tears started falling down Mom's face, like I'd turned on a faucet.

"Do you think she was scared? Do you think she couldn't catch her breath? Do you think she felt scared and couldn't breathe and then . . . just, nothing?"

Now I was crying, too, and then I saw that Dad was

crying. He pulled the car over to the side of the road, and I crawled between the space of the two front seats, and I let Mom and Dad wrap their arms around me, and we all sat like that and cried for a really long time.

Things I Would Tell You about Katie

People kept telling me things like, *Your sister wouldn't want you to be so sad!* Obviously, those people did not know Katie, because she would absolutely want me to be wildly, deeply sad that she died. She would want me to beat my chest and wail. She would want me to feel lost without her. She would want me to feel like the emoji with the exploding head.

Like always, Katie got exactly what she wanted.

Doctor Botticelli
Unofficial Session

Maybe it was thinking that I was dying.

Maybe it was trying to convince Clementine that her sister could have been exposed to trace peanuts in a million ways other than on a knife.

Maybe it was just time.

I mean, isn't that what all the well-meaning people who came to our house during those first horrible days after Katie died kept telling us? *Time heals.* Or some version of that. Mrs. Peabody from the house behind ours told us that it takes a year to get over something like this. "You'll see. Once you've gone through a Thanksgiving and a Christmas and a birthday, once you've experienced every season without her, things will get better." I remember how my mother had looked at her in utter disbelief. "Margaret," Mom had said, "I don't think that I will get over losing my Katie in one year. My baby. I don't think I will get over it in a lifetime."

Mom was right. It had been eight months, and we weren't even close to getting over this. It was unthinkable, impossible to think that we would get over Katie dying like that. But maybe there was some truth in the idea of time passing and changing how you felt.

When Katie first died, it was like an enormous fog of grief descended on me, and I walked around in it and woke up in it, and it was so heavy that sometimes I thought it might suffocate me. Slowly the fog has lifted. Things are sharper and clearer most of the time. Now the sadness is like a cold, hard stone that sits right beside my heart. I can always feel it there. I don't think it will ever go away.

But if I wanted it to get smaller, maybe the size of a pebble, maybe a thing that I'm only aware of sometimes, I needed to come clean about that night. It was too painful to tell Mom and Dad. If I was right, and my shouting *Boo!* killed Katie, they might never forgive me. Or worse, they would forgive me but look at me with such pity that I wouldn't be able to bear being around them.

I wished I had told Clementine about it because

I knew she would have done what all good friends do and tried to convince me that there were other possibilities for the noise that stopped Katie's heart. It might have even made her feel better if she heard herself trying to be reasonable. But I missed my chance that day at Joe's Dairy, and now she wasn't answering my texts.

My next thought was to talk to Gloria at City of Angels. She seemed so capable and sensible, a good person to talk to. But I didn't even know Gloria's last name. I didn't know where to find her, except in that office building where City of Angels met, or on Saturday mornings at Forget-Me-Knot. I didn't want to wait that long.

I went through a list of people, like Ms. Landers and Gilbert and even Granny, but there was always an obstacle to finding them or worry over what their response would be.

Finally, I came to the obvious person: Doctor Botticelli.

I'd been seeing him for months now, and Katie's name hardly came up at all. I knew he was waiting for me to talk about her. Maybe he was waiting for me to confess.

I didn't go to school the day after what I thought of as The Moment When Jude Really, Really Lost It in Front of the Entire School. Mom and Dad thought I should rest.

"Just watch television all day," Dad said, handing me the remote before he went off to work.

Never had I heard those words before from him. Mom and Dad were limit-your-screen-time kind of parents. They liked to make a big bowl of popcorn and force us— me—to watch nature shows. Or give me an hour to watch whatever I wanted, but set a timer so that at exactly one hour that screen went off.

I stayed on the couch all day, under a quilt that smelled like Granny's house, and watched so much TV that I eventually got bored with it. Mom brought me cinnamon toast, and then soup, and later a grilled-cheese-and-bacon sandwich. Every time she came into the room with that food tray, she touched my face and my shoulder like she wanted to be sure I was really there. She touched my forehead and smoothed my hair and adjusted the quilt and watched me eat.

By the next morning, I couldn't wait to leave for school.

Notice I said *leave* for school, not *go* to school, because I had no intention of going to school and having everybody whisper about me and stare at me. I guess I could have called Doctor Botticelli and asked to see him, but I wasn't thinking straight. All I knew was that I couldn't wait for my weekly appointment. No, I was going straight to his office.

It took me almost forever to walk there, and I had to cross Route 2, which was really terrifying because Route 2 is one of those roads lined with stores like Target and Michael's and Best Buy, and restaurants like Chipotle and Subway, and lots of people went to those places, so there were lots of cars and special turn lanes, and let me just say it was very hard to get across that road.

Doctor Botticelli's office in the old Victorian house was down a street off of Route 2, so even after I managed to survive crossing the street, I still had to walk another half mile down a tree-lined, winding road. Also terrifying because of all the curves. Finally, the purple house with Doctor Botticelli's office in it appeared, and I was so relieved to see it that I practically ran up the path to the front door and inside.

Muzak and soft voices came from the closed doors of the other offices. I climbed the stairs to the second floor and took a seat in front of his office. His door was closed, too, which meant he was in there helping some other kid. If that kid just went in, I'd have to sit out here for fifty minutes, which seemed like forever, because I felt like Mount Vesuvius, ready to blow.

Luckily, the door opened in only fifteen minutes, and Doctor Botticelli appeared with a pale boy a lot older than me, probably a senior in high school.

The boy was tall and long limbed and rubbery, and he loped past me without even lifting his head.

"Jude?" Doctor Botticelli said, confused.

"I don't have an appointment," I said.

Before he could tell me to leave or scold me for just showing up, I felt the stone and ash in me building and building. If there were a city below us, I would cover it in ash.

"Whoa," I heard Doctor Botticelli say, and for a moment, I thought maybe stone and ash really were coming out of my head, but then I realized I had somehow gotten to my feet and then opened my mouth, and I was screaming, "Katie! I'm sorry!" And then I was falling into Doctor Botticelli's arms, and he was leading me into his office and pressing me gently onto the loveseat where I liked to sit.

"Tell me," he said.

But I was still screaming.

He was kneeling on the floor in front of me and holding my shoulders with his hairy, knuckled hands and looking straight at me. "Tell me," he said again.

"I killed her," I said, my voice already hoarse from all the screaming. "I killed Katie."

"Jude," he said. "You didn't kill Katie. You didn't."

Oh, I could feel it. All the stone and ash building up and building up, and this time when I opened my mouth, no words came out. I imagined I was spewing volcanic matter. I could see it raining down on Doctor Botticelli and me.

But what really came out of my mouth was a wail that had no end. It went on and on and on, loud and raw and filled with all the pain I had buried deep in my core.

Later, after I was all screamed out, Doctor Botticelli gave me a cup of chamomile tea with honey in it and asked me to tell him everything.

"Everything?" I said, exhausted, because how could I

ever tell anyone everything about Katie? Who she was and what we were like together and all the things we did and all the memories and nicknames and secrets and plans?

"Maybe just everything about that night," he said.

So I told him. I told him every detail, just the way those details had been replaying in my head like they were stuck in some kind of weird loop.

I said:

Around nine o'clock, we stretched out on our beanbags, the ones we got the previous Christmas with our names printed on them, and we held hands and faced each other.

"I don't really want you to drop dead, Jude-o," Katie said.

"I know," I said.

"I'm sorry I read the whole play in one go," she said, with a big sigh. "I couldn't help myself."

"K-k-k-Katie, smarty-pants Katie," I sang softly. She was also Katy-did. Katzenjammer. KK.

"I'm sorry my brother is of inferior intelligence," she said, squeezing my hand.

"Jude of all trades, master of none."

"Do you think I'll ever be a famous actress, JJ?"

"Absolutely."

"And will I win the Pulitzer Prize for Fiction?"

"Most definitely," I said. "Also for Nonfiction. Also the Noble Prize."

"Nobel."

"Huh?"

"My dearest brother. It's No-bel prize. Not No-BUHL. Though it's surely noble to win one," she added kindly.

"But you'll win both. No-bel and No-BUHL."

"Lucky me," Katie said.

"Lucky you," I said, drifting off to sleep.

"Ya lyublyu tebya," Katie said softly.

I smiled. Back in fourth grade, she'd made us both memorize how to say *I love you* in twenty different languages. She'd learned them all, plus ten more.

"Russian," I said sleepily. "Show-off."

Katie stood and pulled me to my feet. She put a hand on the small of my back and led me down the hall to my room. Without asking, she switched on the night-light, knowing I still woke sometimes during the night and was afraid of the dark.

I climbed into bed and managed a "Ti amo."

Katie kissed my hand lightly. "An easy one. But I'll forgive you on the grounds of sleepiness."

I paused.

Doctor Botticelli waited.

"Then I fell asleep, and she went to bed," I said. I could picture the glow of the night-light and Katie turning to go, how the next-to-the-last time I saw her alive, I only glimpsed half of her face, in near darkness.

"Then what?" Doctor Botticelli prodded gently.

"I have this thing, not insomnia exactly, but I wake up in the middle of the night, and I feel scared. That's why I have a night-light. Not Katie though. Nothing woke her up. You know, she slept with her shades open because in case she woke up, she wanted to see the stars or the moon or the sun coming up. She never wanted to miss anything. And now she's missing everything."

"Tell me the rest. You woke up and went to Katie's room?"

"Yeah. It wasn't exactly night. It was dawn; the sky outside her window was mostly gray but kind of streaked with pink and violet. And Katie was sound asleep in her purple striped jammies, holding her old stuffed rabbit, Trixie." I told him how her hair fanned out around her, the open doorway sending in just a small, soft amount of light and Katie and Trixie and her whole room looking so quiet and peaceful and happy, like in "Silent Night" when it goes, *All is calm, all is bright.*

"I stood in the doorway, and instead of whispering her name or even just leaving her alone and letting her sleep, I shouted, 'Boo!' "

I thought I was all cried out, but all of a sudden I was crying again. Not wailing this time, but blubbering like a little kid. I think I was finding all the words for cry.

"I shouted *Boo!* to scare her," I blubbered.

"And that was normal, right, Jude? You two played tricks on each other all the time? Teased each other? Right?"

I nodded.

"So did you?" Doctor Botticelli asked me.

"Did I what?"

"Scare her?"

I looked at him, and he looked at me. My crying slowed, then stopped.

"Did you scare her?" Doctor Botticelli said.

"I . . . I don't know. I mean, no."

He raised his bushy eyebrows. "Of course, it wasn't the middle of the night when you went in, was it? You said it was starting to get light. So when you shouted at her, do you know why she didn't budge?"

I shake my head.

"Why do you think, Jude?" he said so softly.

"I don't know why!"

"Think about it," he said, his voice still soft.

But I was done thinking about it. Done! So I screamed something at Doctor Botticelli, maybe I hate you, or maybe leave me alone, or maybe both, and then I ran out of there as fast as I could.

"I don't want to think about it!" I yelled at the Victorian house, and then I just kept running.

CHAPTER
THIRTY-ONE

When we were little, Katie and I used to play this game she invented. One of us would call out a pasta shape, and the other had to twist their body into that shape. She'd yell, "Fusilli!" and I'd corkscrew to the floor. I'd yell, "Tortellini!" and Katie would curl herself into a circle. I was thinking of that game when I finally got home, limp and droopy. I was overcooked spaghetti.

Would I stop thinking about Katie so much someday? And if that did happen, would it be awful to not have her voice in my head? *Fusilli!*

I barely made it up the stairs to my room, where I flopped onto my bed without even taking off my sneakers. My throat was parched from crying. My eyes stung. I didn't want to talk or think. I just wanted to sleep. So I closed my swollen, burning eyes, and the next thing I knew, the sun was coming through the window at a different angle. My sneakers were off, and my comforter was pulled over me.

Slowly, I realized it was actually morning. I'd slept for something like eighteen hours. My parents were talking in hushed voices, snippets of their conversation floating through the air between us. I closed my eyes again as *poor kid* and *so sad* drifted past. But then I heard something that made me bolt upright. Mom's voice and *Clementine*.

I jumped out of bed and out of my room and ran right to where Mom and Dad sat huddled on the edge of their bed.

They looked surprised to see me.

"What happened?" I said. My voice came out scratchy, and I could smell my own stale breath. "What happened to Clementine?"

Mom looked at Dad, and Dad looked at his hands in his lap.

Then Dad said, "Oh, Jude."

In that moment, it was last year, and the ambulance had taken Katie away, and Dad was about to tell me the worst thing in the world and change my life forever. But this time, I could stop it. If the words did not come out of his mouth, then the worst thing hadn't happened, and Clementine would be okay.

"No!" I said.

"Jude—" Mom began.

I put both my hands up like cartoon people do to stop a speeding train.

"No."

Just like that I turned around and went back to my room.

Their voices started right up again; this time the tone was urgent. My heart was beating fast, so I sat on my bed and took some deep breaths and thought, hard.

I thought about what Doctor Botticelli had said. But sitting there right then, on the edge of my bed, all of that seemed like flimsy logic designed to make me stop feeling like Mount Vesuvius.

I thought about Clementine at Joe's Dairy last week, how certain she was that she did not rinse that knife well enough and Halley used it, and there was trace peanut butter on it, and she died, like the woman who died from her husband's kiss. Because that could always happen, no matter how much we loved someone.

I thought about those two terrible words: *Oh, Jude.*

I thought about how Strawberry Patch didn't let Clementine come home for a long time because they thought she'd do something stupid and terrible again. And I thought about how she told me she'd do something dramatic if she really wanted to hurt herself. Which meant she was maybe making a plan.

I thought about how I hadn't helped her, either. How I had disappointed her. How if I'd just left Katie alone, she might be here still, and I might not even know Clementine or City of Angels or Forget-Me-Knot or any of the things that made up my sad life.

Then I stood up, dumped all of my school stuff out of my backpack, filled it with the things I'd need, and slipped out of my house, all while my parents tried to figure out what to do next.

Jude Banks, Superhero

Officer Jeffers said, "I'm not going to book you."

He looked over my shoulder and nodded at something behind me. When I turned around, I saw my parents rushing toward me.

Mom grabbed my shoulders and said, "I'm so mad at you!" then pulled me close to her and said, "I love you so much, Jude."

From beneath my mother's bony arms, I asked her how they even found me.

"Your name and phone number are on your backpack," Officer Jeffers said. "Easy police work."

Then he told us to all come into his office.

He had a messy desk and uncomfortable chairs, and it was too small for four people, but we all crowded in there.

"Your kid thinks he murdered someone," Officer Jeffers

said, no preliminaries, just like a TV cop.

"Sweetie," Mom said, "Doctor Botticelli tried explaining everything to you. But you ran out before he could finish."

"You know that I saw him yesterday?" I said, surprised.

"Of course we know," she said. "He called us as soon as you left. He was worried about you."

"But what about Clementine?" I said, my head kind of spinning.

"Clementine called Gloria at City of Angels and said she needed to go back to Strawberry Patch because she couldn't stop thinking that hurting herself was the only way to feel better," Dad said.

"She said that she'd talked to you about what happened to her sister and that you were sensible and kind, and when even that didn't stop her from feeling guilty, she called Gloria," Mom said.

"She's not dead?" I said.

"No, sweetie," Mom said.

"You saved her life, Jude," Dad said.

"I did?" I said, trying to let this good news sink in.

"She wants you to visit her on Saturday," Mom said.

"So I thought we'd all take a ride to the Cape? Maybe get lobster rolls after you see Clementine?"

I made myself repeat the words *Clementine is not dead* until I actually believed them. Clementine was not dead, and I had saved her life. And I would get to see her on Saturday. I could feel tears stinging my eyes, but they were happy tears.

"We'll bring her a jigsaw puzzle," I said. "She likes doing them."

Officer Jeffers was asking if we were all okay, and Mom and Dad were thanking him, but I wasn't really listening. Instead, things were clicking into place, like when Katie and I used to build those elaborate LEGO models, Ferris wheels and the Louvre.

Clementine was alive.

I started thinking about Pompeii again. One of the victim's brains actually turned to glass from being vaporized. I didn't understand the science, but it was true. His brain turned to glass. That was what was happening to me, I thought, as I realized what Doctor Botticelli had been trying to get me to say yesterday. My brain was like glass. I could think clearly for the first time since Dad walked into the kitchen after the EMTs took Katie away.

I closed my eyes and pictured me standing in Katie's doorway. I heard myself yell *Boo!* And then I stood there, waiting for her to wake up and yell at me. I stood there. I waited. I said, "Katie?" And she didn't move. She didn't move.

Instead of that pressure building that felt like ash and stones, I suddenly felt light, like I could lift out of this uncomfortable chair and fly around this room, around this whole police station, and out the door. Light.

Dad was signing some papers now. Mom was talking, her lips moving at Officer Jeffers.

"Dad," I said, tugging on his arm. "Dad. When they did the autopsy, they figured out that Katie had died before Mom ground the coffee, right?"

Dad turned toward me. "It happened some time between eleven and two," he said. "While we were all asleep."

I could see that dawn light out Katie's window, and it was almost as if it was washing over me right now. That's what Doctor Botticelli was trying to get me to realize. She didn't budge because she had already died, hours before.

"Me too," I said. "I was asleep, too."

The voice that came out was strong and true. It was my voice.

Mom had turned toward me, too, and somewhere behind all the sadness on her face, I saw the other her, the real Mom. She was still in there.

∾⊥∽

It was Mom who suggested we go to Joe's Dairy and get some lunch.

"I'm famished," she said.

Famished was such a typical Mom word that I started to laugh. Mom and Dad glanced at each other with a *Boy, is he weird* look and that made me feel so good that I actually blurted, "I love you guys."

They looked at each other again.

"We love you, too, buddy," Dad said.

We drove past one of the playgrounds Dad had designed. It was for little kids under the age of five, so everything was small and adorable. I hadn't even noticed what a bright, sunny day it was, but when I saw all those little kids running around Dad's playground in shorts and T-shirts, I realized that it was practically summer.

I rolled down the window and let in the warm June air and the squeals of those kids having fun. In one section of the playground, there were all these hidden water jets that sent water out in zigzags that kids could run through. I wished I was under five and could go and run through the water with them.

"After lunch, we can stop at a bookstore so you can get Clementine a puzzle," Mom said when we sat down in one of the red booths at Joe's Dairy.

We all picked up the menus and studied them, even though we knew them by heart.

I got my usual hot dog, and Mom and Dad both got Joe's cheeseburger with everything. "All the way," Dad called it.

It felt so normal being there together, except for the big missing piece called Katie. I knew we all had a long way to go before we got back to our ordinary lives, but I knew, too, that something had shifted, that we were on our way back, anyway.

"What is in this sauce?" Mom said as she chewed her burger.

Dad and I laughed. Mom always wondered what was in Joe's special sauce. Once, she offered twenty dollars to the cook if he'd tell her, but he said he didn't know, either. Only Joe's family knew.

"Definitely ketchup," Mom said. "And mayo? But what else?"

I watched her frowning and thinking and eating, and Dad beside her smiling the way he did when he was amused by her. Then I whipped my cape around me, the red one with the sparkly *J*. I lifted up into the air and looked down at Mom and Dad and my regular self, Jude Banks. I saw a family sitting there. And my broken heart filled with so much love that it covered everything and everybody. I'd been trying so hard to save the world from pain that I'd forgotten to save myself.

The family sat there in that red booth, and I smiled down at them. I spread my arms, and my cape fluttered in the breeze. My job was done. But theirs—that family of three—was just beginning.

ACKNOWLEDGMENTS

In 2002, my five-year-old daughter, Grace, died suddenly and my world, and my family's world, was turned upside down. Ever since then, I've struggled to write about grief, and to help others understand and manage grief. My son, Sam, was nine when his sister Grace died. He was her friend, her co-conspirator, and the best big brother a girl could have. Just as we were lucky to have had Grace in our lives, she was lucky to have Sam for a brother. And I am the luckiest mom to have Sam as my son. Thanks to him here for always making me smile, loving me so fiercely as I do him, and being the kid I always dreamed of having. The same is true of my daughter Annabelle, who is the Rory to my Lorelai, the baby bear to my mama bear, the best daughter and friend any mom has had. She reads what I write and gives me honest critiques. She shares her ideas with me for revisions (and told me my first draft was boring!). And Jude wouldn't exist without her feedback. Thank you isn't big enough for these two special people, or for my fabulous husband, Michael, the love of my life. My love for all of them has no bounds.

Thank you too to Nathaniel Tabachnik, who works tirelessly and with such good humor. Thanks to everyone at Penguin Workshop for believing in me and believing in this story. And thank you with all my heart to the amazing Francesco Sedita, who tells me to write what's in my heart, and helps me do just that. He is every writer's dream editor, and I'm glad he's mine.

Photo credit: Tracey Minkin

ANN HOOD is the author of the novel *She Loves You (Yeah, Yeah, Yeah)* and fourteen books for adults. She lives in Providence, Rhode Island, with her husband, her daughter Annabelle, and their two cats, Hermia and Gertrude.